A
Swe
Ros

CW00727354

The battle to trust and communicate, fan the flames in Nia and Derek's already over-heated relationship. It's their way, a way back to one another.

A way back is further complicated by a constant threat to Nia's safety. There is a traitor in their midst. Friendships are tested and broken, and Nia's choices cause irreversible damage.

Their road to freedom and happiness is rough and terrifying, but it is the only way home.

A WAY BACK
Swept Away, Book 3

ROSEMARY WILLHIDE

LUMINOSITY PUBLISHING LLP

A WAY BACK
Swept Away, Book 3
Copyright © March 2015 Rosemary Willhide
ISBN: 978-1-910397-61-9

Cover Art by Poppy Designs

ALL RIGHTS RESERVED

No part of this literary work may be reproduced in any form or by any means, including electronic or photographic reproduction, in whole or in part, without the written permission of the publisher.

This is a work of fiction. All characters and events in this book are fictitious. Any resemblance to actual persons living or dead is purely coincidental.

The author acknowledges the trademark status and the following trademark owners mentioned in this work of fiction:

Google, Facebook, Jell-O, Crock-Pot, Saran Wrap, Tupperware, Pyrex, Ben & Jerry's, Hallmark

Dedication

This book is dedicated to the love of my life, my husband, William Patrick Johnson. There isn't a chance in hell I could've done any of this without you. When I started this journey, I didn't even know how to copy and paste. You held my hand and helped me every step of the way. I love you. This one is for you. Thank you for being my everything. From our very first kiss, I knew, with you, I was home.

Chapter One

"Please, Nia, you have to eat something. You can't teach on an empty stomach." Brooke was in my office, attempting to get food into me.

It had been three weeks, three weeks since I saw Derek kissing Mandy Hamilton in his trailer—three weeks since he let go.

I grazed my fingers over the wrapper of the protein bar. "Tomorrow is Derek's birthday."

"I know. I can't believe you haven't heard from him."

"I can. The look on his face when he saw my engagement ring sitting on the kitchen island said it all. He was done. I miss him, but after what happened with Mandy…I don't see a way back from that."

"Are you sure? You never gave him a chance to explain."

"What's there to explain? I saw it with my own eyes. Mandy stripped her top off in his trailer. I know they were rehearsing, but still. I keep asking myself what would've happened if I hadn't walked in to surprise Derek with lunch that day. How far would things have gone?"

"I'm sorry. You're right. It's just hard to imagine what Derek was thinking. He loved you so much."

"He did love me, but not enough to say no to Hollywood. That was never going to change."

"I wish there was something I could do."

I opened up the protein bar and took a bite. "Are you kidding? You're doing everything for me. Thank you for letting Molly and me stay at your house. You've been taking great care of both of us."

"I love having you. With Tom out of town it's a win-win for both of us."

"I really appreciate it. I couldn't impose on Julia and Phillip. It's only been a month since she had the miscarriage."

"Yeah, but I'm glad they're spending so much time together. As far as I can tell, it's brought them closer together."

Jake popped his head in the doorway. "Sorry to interrupt. I was just wondering when I could drive you home today, Nia."

Even though Derek and I broke up, Jake was still my driver and bodyguard. It was a constant reminder of Derek and Larry Wall. Larry's parole hearing was less than a week away. He could be getting out of jail. He could be coming after me.

"Actually, Jake, you have the night off. Brooke's going to drive me, and I'm going to teach Lacey's private class tonight."

His sparkling green eyes narrowed. "I'm afraid I don't understand."

Brooke flashed him a sheepish grin. "You will

when you text your girlfriend, Lacey."

Jake cleared his throat. "Oh, I see. Thank you. I will pick you up tomorrow morning at the usual time?"

"Yes, eight o'clock. Have a great night."

Jake hurried out with a skip in his step.

I exhaled. "Yeah, it's all so romantic those first few months. Is it just me, or does falling in love suck the life out of you?"

"It's just you, for now. You won't feel this way forever."

"Won't I?"

"Nia, I know it doesn't seem like it right now, but one of these days you will fall in love again. After my divorce, I thought I was destined to be single, and now I'm happier than ever."

"I doubt it. My heart's closed for good. My walls are up so high you'd need a load of dynamite to get them down."

"I get that. It's exactly how I felt. But time really does heal all wounds. In the meantime, could you do two things for me?"

"Of course. Name it."

Brooke took my hands in hers. "I think you need to have a good cry. You haven't shed a single tear."

I hung my head. "I shed all my tears in LA. There aren't any left. I'm afraid I can't do that for you. What else you got?"

"You need to take better care of yourself. You haven't been eating enough. You've lost a lot of weight. I'm worried about you."

"I'm just not hungry."

"But you need to eat more. If you don't, I'm afraid I will have to resort to extreme measures."

"What extreme measures?"

Brooke smiled. "I'll tell Julia."

I grabbed the protein bar and crammed it into my mouth. Brooke laughed.

After I finished, I said, "Wow! You really played hardball. And, you're right, I don't look very healthy. I should set a good example. Maybe after tomorrow I'll turn a corner. Derek's birthday has been weighing on me. I was thinking about going to his house tomorrow and picking up my stuff."

"That's a good idea. It'll be a big step in moving on."

"I don't really want to walk in that house again. All of my memories of Derek will come flooding back, but I have to."

"I'll go with you if you want."

"No, that's okay. I need to do this alone. I just have to figure out a way to give Jake the slip."

"Tell him I'm going with you. If you need to go to Derek's by yourself then you should do it. I bet you'll start to feel better the next day. You might even get your appetite back."

Walter James appeared in the doorway, sweaty from his private spin class.

"Hey, Nia, I wanted to tell you Christa is doing a

great job. I miss taking class with you, but you should know you've got yourself a top-notch instructor."

"Thanks, Walter, that's good to hear. Is Christa in the fitness room?"

"Yeah, she asked me to tell you she needed to talk to you about something."

"Okay, I'm on my way. Brooke, I'll see you after class."

I hightailed it to the fitness room to talk to Christa. Christa Howard was in her thirties with long, auburn hair. I didn't have the opportunity to chat with her much. She was quite the hustler, traveling from gym to gym. She taught over twenty classes a week. How did she squeeze them all in? Her infectious grin made her popular with the members. Her toned, curvy figure probably made her popular with men.

"Hey, Christa, you needed to talk to me?"

She shut the door. "Yeah, I hope I'm not overstepping. But you've been on my mind. I wanted to say how sorry I am about you and Derek. You were such a beautiful couple."

I stared at the floor, not relishing the conversation. "I guess it just wasn't meant to be."

She sauntered toward me with a twinkle in her dark eyes. "If it's not too personal, can I ask who broke up with who?"

My fingers rubbed my temples in frustration. "I suppose, at the end of the day, I broke up with him. I don't like to talk about it."

"I'm sorry, I didn't mean to pry. Is it okay if I give you a hug?"

A hug? What could I say? "Oh, sure."

Christa wrapped her arms around me. She held me tight, a little too tight. Her full breasts pressed against me. The floral scent of her hair permeated my nose. She broke our embrace, and grasped my face. Her lips puckered in a sly smile. Without warning, she brought her mouth to mine and kissed me. Her lips were so soft and gentle. *What the fuck? Am I a lesbian now?* She expelled a faint moan.

I snapped my head away from hers. "Um...what are you doing there?"

"Nia, I'm sorry. You can fire me if you want to, but I've been wanting to do that for a really long time."

"Well...huh...that's flattering...I guess. I didn't know you were... It doesn't matter. I just didn't know you were gay."

"I'm not gay. I choose not to limit myself. There are so many pleasures to enjoy. I want to experience everything."

My eyes darted about the room. "I suppose it's nice to have options."

She chuckled. "Yes, I like my options. Not every woman turns me on, but you do. I think you're so sexy, and you have a great ass."

My hands clutched my bum in protection. "Oh, thanks... Your ass is nice too, but—"

She ran her fingers through my hair. "Before you

finish that sentence, just hear me out. I know you're not over Derek, but I could make you feel good. We could just play. You wouldn't have to touch me if you're uncomfortable. It would be about me pleasing you. I would love to taste you."

This was so not happening, and yet I didn't want to hurt her feelings or embarrass her. "That's…you know, very generous of you. I'm going to go with, no, but thanks."

Her lips brushed my cheek. "I understand. If you ever change your mind, I'm here. In fact, can I make a little confession?"

"I see no reason to stop now."

"I used to fantasize about doing a three-way with you and Derek. When it comes to sex, I say the more the merrier. Am I freaking you out?"

"No, not at…" I swallowed nervously. "Yes, you're freaking me out a little. But please don't think I'm passing judgment. I say, you do you, and whoever else you like. I'm just not wired that way."

"That's cool. I hope it won't be weird, now that I've kissed you."

"No, you're actually a really good kisser."

She laughed. "That's a relief. I tend to come on a little strong."

"The crazy thing is, a small part of me wishes I was more like you. Maybe I wouldn't be so heartbroken."

"It's Derek's loss. Even if you did break up with him, I can't believe he isn't in Vegas fighting for you."

"I guess neither one of us had any fight left."

"I'm sorry. I'd better go, so you can get ready for your private. Just to make sure, you and I are cool, right?"

"Yes, we're cool. Actually, I should give you a raise. You took Walter James off my hands for good. He says you're a top-notch instructor."

"Ah, sweet! I like Walter. I think he's a great guy."

She thought Walter was a great guy? I did pass judgment on that, just a smidge.

* * * *

I was on the front steps of Derek's house on his thirty-third birthday. Originally, I planned to fly to LA for a birthday surprise. Surely, he had a big Hollywood bash to attend in his honor. Did he ever think about me, about us?

With shaky fingers, I pushed the key into the lock, and the door drifted ajar. It was as if I opened up a fairy tale with a heartbreaking ending.

The first thing that hit me was the way the house smelled. It was a familiar scent of fresh linens and happy moments. It smelled like home.

I trudged up the stairs to collect my things. When I landed in the bedroom, my jaw quivered uncontrollably. Perhaps Brooke would get her wish. Tears threatened my eyes. I plopped on the bed, plucked up Derek's pillow, clutched it to my chest, and rocked myself back and forth.

"Please, God, I can't cry. If I start, I won't ever stop."

My body trembled giving way to the inevitable. I buried my face in Derek's pillow. A slight sob escaped and the floodgates opened. I curled up in a ball and wept on the bed. It was our bed. A place where we made love so many times I lost count. He swept me away in this very room. He swept me a way to our bubble, our safe place—our sanctuary.

I convulsed in agony as the tears flowed. I was a fool to think I was strong enough to come here and collect my things, as if I was over him. I still loved Derek. I loved him so much. I didn't know how to stop loving him.

This was a mistake. *I have to get out of here.* I could come back another day, with Brooke.

"Nia."

I jerked up and found Derek standing before me. His face bore the same somber expression I carried for weeks. I pressed my lips together to squelch my quaking jaw.

I found my voice and said quietly, "I know I shouldn't be here. I just came to pick up my stuff. I promise I'll leave. I shouldn't be here."

Derek's gaze captured mine. "Baby, where else would you be? This is your home."

There wasn't a single shred of strength in me. My body caved in on itself. I lost control and sobbed.

Without a moment's hesitation Derek rushed to my side and gathered me to his lap.

He crushed me to his chest. "Shh... My sweet girl. It's going to be all right. I'm going to make this all right. Please give me a chance to make this all right."

I melted into him while his words swirled in my head. I couldn't take them in. All I could do was relish his touch and his scent. It was like giving water to someone dying of thirst. Eventually the tears subsided and my breathing calmed.

"Sweetie, look at me."

I peeked up at him and stared into those beautiful blue eyes, full of hope and regret.

The back of his hand caressed my cheek. "I missed you."

He brought his mouth to mine. My lips opened to him and granted him access. His essence overwhelmed me. His lips were in a frenzy devouring my neck, my mouth, my very soul. I traced my fingertips over every contour of his face, committing it to memory, his strong jaw line, the bridge of his nose. Was he real? He consumed me as if he was starving. The sound of our heaving breath resonated in the room. What was I doing? Nothing had changed. Nothing would ever change.

"Derek, stop. I can't do this."

He clutched my face in his hands. "I can't stop. I won't ever stop. I came back to fight for you. Please, give me another chance. Let me hold you in the tub and explain."

I wriggled off his lap and stood. "There's nothing left to explain."

"There is so much you don't know. I've been working like a dog, trying to figure this out so we can be together. You have to believe me, sweetie."

My voice shook. "Please don't call me that. I can't take it."

He came to me and grasped me by the shoulders. "I can't take living without you. It's eating me alive. I love you. You are mine, and I am yours. We belong together."

"But you let go. You promised, no matter what, you would never let go. You let go."

I shrugged him off and dashed for the hallway. His footsteps thudded behind me. I flew down the stairs to the door. I couldn't look back. I would splinter in two if I did.

He shouted after me. "Nia, I'm not giving up. I will never give up on us."

Chapter Two

After I cried myself to sleep last night, I soldiered on to work with Molly in tow. My little black puppy—who wasn't so little anymore—was a constant source of comfort. I nicknamed her my hip pocket. She followed me everywhere like a dutiful friend. Today she would be my security blanket of joy. She never ceased to make me smile.

As we trotted through the door of the country club, Shannon paced the floor.

Once she spotted Molly and me, she raced to my side. "I've been trying to reach you. I left you like a thousand messages."

"Sorry, I saw Derek last night, so I turned my phone off."

"Derek's in town?"

"Yeah, but it's a mess. I can't talk about it. Why did you leave me so many messages?"

"I was trying to warn you. Someone's waiting for you in your office. I tried to get rid of her, but she demanded to see you."

"Is it Sonya Reed? Should we call the police?"

"No. It's your stepmother."

My stomach sickened instantly. What the fuck was Evelyn doing here? "Seriously, my stepmother is in my office?"

"Yes. She's a psycho! One second she was kissing my ass with compliments, and the next she threatened me if I didn't let her in your office."

"That is vintage step-mommy dearest. I should get this over with."

"Do you want me to call someone? This woman is looney tunes. Maybe I should call Brooke, or...Derek?"

"No! Don't call anyone. Especially not Derek. Come on, Molly, it's time to look pure evil in the face."

Molly and I made our way to my office. Before my eyes fell upon Evelyn, my nose recognized the reeking stench of her signature, cheap-ass perfume.

Molly let out a shrill bark that jerked Evelyn out of her seat. Her voice dripped with soured honey. "Oh, there you are." She looked me up and down with her stony, disapproving glare. "My, don't you look well."

My spine straightened. "What are you doing here, Evelyn? I told you never to contact me again."

She plastered on her fake smile and hit me with the danger tone. It couldn't be trusted. "Oh, don't be silly. I felt terrible how we left things. I thought long and hard about what you said. And, you're right. Maybe all these years I've treated you unfairly. Perhaps I was even a little jealous. I'm here to make amends."

My stepmother didn't make amends. She made trouble.

Molly jumped up on Evelyn, causing her to stumble. "You bring your dog to work?"

"Yes, Molly comes everywhere with me. I know you're allergic to dogs, but she's not leaving."

I plopped down a new toy for Molly and she went to work on destroying it.

Evelyn settled back in her chair. "That's fine. I'm not allergic any more."

"How convenient." I sat and stared her dead in the eyes. "You flew across the country to make amends? Let's not kid ourselves. You don't like me, and I don't like you. What's really going on here?"

The real Evelyn slipped through a little. "I don't appreciate your accusing tone."

"I don't appreciate you showing up where I work, unannounced. So either tell me what this is really about, or I'll call security and have them escort you off the premises. It's your call."

It was then I took a good long look at her. When she first entered my life, her grand ways and imposing posture intimidated me. Today, she appeared smaller than I remembered. Her deep frown lines and pale skin showed signs of a chink in her rigid armor.

She bunched up her fists, and exhaled. "Fine. I've gotten myself into a bit of hot water. I was hoping you could help me. Not for me, but for the girls. You're my last hope. Do you still have your father's inheritance?"

"You came all this way for money? How could you be out of money? Dad was a great provider."

She drew her lips into a hard line. "Just answer the question. Do you have the money, or don't you?"

"No, I don't have the money. I already wrote to you months ago and told you most of it went to a charity I started."

"Well, what about your rich fiancé? He probably has more money than you could ever spend."

The pad of my thumb brushed over my vacant ring finger. Somehow, we managed to keep our breakup out of the press. I heard rumblings that Mandy put out a story saying she came between us, but Derek released a statement debunking her claims. I couldn't let Evelyn discover the truth.

This was like a game of chess. "Why don't you tell me what happened, and I'll see what I can do."

"I made a bad investment. All the money your father left me is gone. I have the house, but I can't make ends meet."

She unclenched her fists. My eyes fell on her perfectly manicured nails. She saw me spy them and said, "I'm telling you the truth. I got a job at a salon. It doesn't pay much, but I get my hair and nails done for free."

It was difficult to picture Evelyn working. She was more of the type to prattle on about how busy she was, even though she had zero demands on her time.

I appreciated her earnest effort to get a job, and yet I wasn't completely satisfied. "I believe you, about the job. I'd like to know why you risked everything for one investment."

She let her guard down. "Peter assured me it would

pay off handsomely."

"Peter? As in Peter Hanson from the neighborhood? Why in the world would you trust him with anything? Dad couldn't stand him."

Peter Hanson openly flirted with Evelyn at every neighborhood get-together. She ate it up like a lovelorn teenager.

The pieces of this fucked-up puzzle were fitting together. "Are you involved romantically with Peter Hanson?"

Evelyn contemplated her next move. "I was very lonely after your father died."

"Answer the question."

"The truth is, I was involved with him."

"It's only been five months. Out of respect for Dad, couldn't you have waited, or at the very least not fucked Peter Hanson."

She jumped up. "Don't you dare speak to me like that with your foul mouth, *Meagan*."

I leaned back calmly in my chair, ready for checkmate. "It's my office. I'll speak to you any way I want. If you don't like it, leave."

"Are you sure that's how you want to play it? I hear the tabloids pay plenty of money for juicy stories. I can see the headlines now. 'Derek Pierce's fiancée leaves her father's widow penniless.' Or better yet, 'The secret breakup of Derek Pierce and his fiancée.' I know Derek denied it in the paper, but that empty ring finger tells a different story. You've got two choices.

Give me the money, or I'll make your life a living hell in the press."

"You actually are pure evil. Why my dad saw any good in you is beyond me. I'm calling security. You're getting out of my life for good."

"Go ahead, call security. You've just told me everything I need to know. You and the great Derek Pierce did breakup. It's written all over your face. I knew you wouldn't be able to hang onto him. He's too good for you."

I snapped to my feet ready to charge her when Derek burst through the door. "Sorry to interrupt. Sweetie, you left this morning without your engagement ring."

What the hell was he doing? Beads of sweat formed on my brow. Molly went bonkers. She hadn't seen him for weeks. She whimpered and cried.

Derek played it off. "Molly, I just saw you this morning, silly girl. He bent down to pet her. She calmed immediately.

He rose and touched his lips to my forehead. "Here, angel, here's your ring."

He slipped the ring on my finger, just as he did when he proposed. Only now my hand trembled. Derek squeezed it in a gentle, reassuring manner. I made the mistake of glancing up at him. The love in his eyes for me nearly knocked me off my feet.

I stared at the floor. "Thank you. Thank you for bringing it. I'll try to be more careful. Um…Derek, this is my stepmother, Evelyn Michaels. Evelyn, this is my fiancé, Derek Pierce."

Evelyn laid it on thick. "It's such an honor to meet you, Mr. Pierce."

Derek regarded her coldly. "Thank you. What brings you to Vegas?"

A nervous laugh trickled from her pinched face. "Why Nia, of course. It's been ages."

"Evelyn, seriously, cut the shit," I said with my anger back in tow. "Derek, she's here for money. She fucked it all away to some loser my dad hated. Now she's threatening to drag us through the tabloids."

Her face flushed in sheer embarrassment. "I don't know where you got such a wild story. I only came to… to… Yes, I'm strapped. I'm working my fingers to the bone to provide for my daughters. It just isn't enough."

Derek took a step in her direction. "How much would be enough? How much would it take for you to leave Nia alone for good?"

Her eyes grew wide. "What are you saying? You want me to give you a number?"

I interrupted, "Derek, you don't have to do this. I can deal with it. I've been dealing with *her* my entire life."

"Nia, it's fine. I would like Evelyn to give me a number, because I don't want her to bother you ever again. Do you have the country club's checkbook?"

"It's in my desk. Why?"

"May I have it? I'm going to write your stepmother

a check, you sign it, and she can be on her way. I'll replace the money in their account. It will only take a quick text to my business manager."

Gripped with indecision, I clutched onto the desk. Should I let Derek pay her off? We aren't even together. I couldn't lead him on.

Derek leaned down and whispered in my ear, "Please let me do this. Don't argue with me, baby."

His warm breath against my skin broke me out in goose flesh. I exhaled. "Are you sure you can replace it right away? I shook my head as a sign to say this didn't change anything. "I don't want to…to get in trouble."

He caressed my face and held my gaze. "It's all going to be okay. I promise."

I gave him the checkbook. He veered his attention to Evelyn. "So, what's it going to be?"

When she was nervous or trapped, her chest would breakout in tiny red dots. Evelyn appeared to have a serious case of the measles. "Well, that's very generous of you. I suppose fifty thousand dollars would help a great deal."

"Fifty thousand dollars!" I blurted. "Are you out of your mind? Derek, you can't give her fifty thousand dollars. It's ridiculous."

Derek splayed his hand on the small of my back, almost making my knees fold beneath me. "Sweetheart, let me handle this." With a flourish, he opened the checkbook. "Evelyn, should I make this out to cash?"

"That would work."

Derek continued, "I'm going to make you a deal. Today you'll leave here with a check for five thousand dollars. If you leave Nia alone, and don't plant any stories in the press, next month you can look forward to another five grand. Just know, if you attempt to contact her in anyway, the deal is off. Once the fifty thousand is paid in full, you will not get another dime from us. Are we clear?"

"Yes. Thank you for doing this for me."

I signed it and Derek handed her the check. "I'm not doing it for you. I'm doing it for Nia."

She folded the check and stuffed it in her purse. "I don't know what to say."

He gestured toward the door. "You should say goodbye. You need to leave."

Evelyn was at a loss. She threw me a quick look —"Thank you, Nia. I promise you will never hear from me again. Goodbye"—and scampered out the door.

Derek shut the door and fired off a quick text.

I stayed behind the desk as if it was my protection. Was he going to keep fighting for me?

"You shouldn't have done that. You don't owe me anything. How did you know my stepmother was here?"

"Shannon called me."

"I specifically asked her not to."

"Please don't be angry with her. She did the right thing. Your stepmother is a horrible human being."

"You're right. She is. I suppose I should be grateful

to you. I mean, I am. Thank you."

"Can we talk? I just need five minutes. Let's sit on the floor together with Molly."

I stood motionless. I couldn't be ripped open again like last night. It was too much.

"Sweetie, look at me. Come here. Just five minutes."

Derek and I sat across from each other, by my desk on the floor. Molly dove in between us. She wagged her tail with vigor. She missed us being a family. Deep down I missed it too.

I gazed into his ice-blue eyes and tears welled up. He was supposed to be my husband someday. He was supposed to be my forever.

I covered my face with my hands and sighed. Derek took them in his. "I don't want to spring anything on you. I want to make a plan, a plan for tomorrow night. I'm going to talk and you're going to listen. After you hear me out, if you really think we're through, then I'll walk out of your life for good. I came back here to fight for you, but I'm willing to let you go if that's what you really want. I hated to see you cry like that last night. But I really believe we still have a chance. Please, give us a chance."

"It's not that I don't want to give us a chance. It's that... It's just...if we break up again. I don't think I'm strong enough to survive it. I barely survived this time."

"What you're doing isn't surviving. You're existing. When I saw you last night, it broke me to see how tiny you are. Baby, you look like you haven't eaten a thing since you left LA. I need to take care of you."

"I'm doing better. At least I promised Brooke I would try, but then I saw you, and it all came flooding back. I had images of Mandy flying through my head. I just got them out. I don't want to go back. I want to move on. It's the right thing. It's the safe thing, for me."

"I know you better than you know yourself. Your walls are up, just like when we met. You're protecting yourself. But if you just hear me out, I can change it."

I withdrew my hands from his. "You don't understand. I'm the one who changed. Seeing you with Mandy changed me. I'm bitter and so fucking angry. I can't change that. I don't know how. I'm not the same girl you fell in love with. I'm not your girl anymore."

Derek leaned in. "That's not true. You don't mean that."

I picked myself up off the floor. "I do mean that. There's no point in hearing you out, because I won't be able to hear you. My anger will block it out, and I can't cry anymore. I can't keep doing this to myself."

He flew to his feet in protest. "What about what this has done to me? Do you ever think about that at all? You're not the only one who is just existing. I can't sleep anymore, because you're not in my arms. My arms were made to hold you and protect you and love you. Now they're empty."

His six-foot-four frame towered over me. "Nia,

listen to what I have to say. It doesn't have to be tomorrow night. I'll settle for any night. Please."

It was too big a gamble. As much as I loved him, I couldn't erase him and Mandy from my mind. It would eat at me for the rest of my life. It was my turn to let go. I slipped the ring off my finger and placed it in his hand. "I'm sorry. I can't. I think you should go."

Chapter Three

"Nia Kelly, you are going out tonight and I'm not taking no for an answer." Julia was in full Julia mode on the phone. Why did I even answer it?

"I'm sorry. I'm just not up for it. I'll come over if you want. Brooke could probably use a break from me."

"We are all going out. It'll be good for us. You and I have been a couple of hermits."

"I hear you and I'm glad you're doing better, I really am. You sound like yourself again, but I'm just not ready, especially after seeing Derek yesterday.

"Please, Nia, do this for me. Phillip's out of town for the first time since the miscarriage. I need to get out of this house, and have some fun. It's been forever since we had a girls' night."

Julia was right, again. It would be good for us. I relented. "Okay, I'm in. What's the plan?"

"Drinks and dinner at the country club. Jake is driving all of us, so we can get turned up."

"So, Jake knew before I did? Wow! You really worked this one. Was he going to kidnap me if I said no?"

She laughed. "That was plan B. See you at seven."

* * * *

As Julia, Brooke, Lacey, and I made our way to the bar at the clubhouse, we stopped to visit with the Petersons, the chorus girls, and their husbands at a corner table for six. They had been there since happy hour and were quite happy indeed. The way the husbands flirted with their wives was charming. They'd all been married over twenty years and still had that spark with each other. It was what I longed for with Derek. Maybe coming to the country club wasn't such a great idea. This place held so many memories.

Lacey waved her hand in front of my face. "Earth to Nia."

"I'm sorry. I spaced out for a second."

"Are you thinking about Derek?" Julia asked.

"Yeah. He wanted to get together and talk tonight. I just couldn't do it. But I can't stop thinking about him."

Brooke grabbed my hand. "Well then, it's safe to say we made the right decision. Girls, shall we?"

Lacey and Julia placed their drinks on the bar. The three of them led me out the door and down the hall. It was like a police escort, only they were more firm and brutal. "Will someone please tell me what is going on? I don't like surprises."

Brooke unlocked the private dining room, while Lacey and Julia strengthened their grip on me.

"Seriously, someone better tell me what the hell you all are up to."

"For once, could you just go with the flow?" Julia griped.

The girls practically shoved me inside, and Brooke slammed the door shut.

"Thank you, ladies. I appreciate it," Derek said with his gaze fixed on me.

I should have known. This was all his doing. My friends threw me under the bus and backed over me ten times.

"I don't appreciate it. This is a total ambush. I'm leaving."

Lacey and Brooke blocked the door.

I looked to Julia and pleaded, "I know your heart was in the right place, but please."

"Nia, you need to give him a chance to explain. Once you hear what Derek told me last night, you will change your mind."

"He told you?"

"Yes, because you were too stubborn to listen."

I glanced in Derek's direction and my heart sped up. He sauntered to us in his commanding stride and gave Julia a kiss on the cheek. "Again, thank you. All of you. Dinner and drinks are on me tonight. Enjoy."

My turncoats left. They left me alone with Derek. This wasn't fair.

"Just because you bribe my friends with booze and fancy food doesn't mean I have to listen to a word you say."

I headed for the door and Derek hoisted me over

his shoulder. "Yes it does. I'm going to talk and you're going to listen." He deposited me in a chair.

I immediately shot out of my seat. "No, I'm not."

Derek threw his hands in the air in frustration. "You are the most exasperating woman on the planet. God, you make me crazy. Do you know that?"

"If I am, then what I am doing here? Why did you orchestrate this whole thing, if I make you so crazy?"

He clutched me to him. "Because I'm so fucking in love with you."

His lips crashed to mine. He took my mouth with such force it knocked the wind out of me. The palms of my hands pushed against his brick-like chest. I couldn't succumb to the power his very being had over me. My resistance fueled his fiery determination. He growled into my mouth, and I dizzied from head to toe. I was losing control.

He released me, and for a moment our eyes locked on one another while we caught our breath. His hands cupped my face. "Please, my angel, please."

I nodded and sank into the chair. A slight smile curved on his lips as he pulled a chair close to mine and took a seat.

"Thank you, sweetie. For starters, I'm sorry for what you saw in my trailer that day. It wasn't what it looked like."

"I know what I saw."

"I know how it must've seemed, but right before you got there we were rehearsing in front of everyone and Mandy said she was uncomfortable and asked if we could rehearse in private. It was stupid of me to agree, and the only reason I suggested my trailer was because I foolishly thought I could control the situation. Once we were away from everyone, it was clear she made the request just to be alone with me. So, the first few times we rehearsed the scene, I did a line reading with her, nothing more. Then she went off. She said I was holding back because I didn't find her attractive and maybe she should quit. I didn't want the show to go down because of me, so I suggested we try it again. That's what you walked in on."

"I don't see how that changes anything. There's always a Mandy, or a Lena waiting around the corner. You had a choice to make that day. You could've stood up for yourself and for us when she asked to rehearse in private, and you didn't. It's always going to be that way, and if that's the way you want to live your life that's fine, but I don't. I can't."

"I don't want either one of us to live like that. I've realized I need to put you first and to hell with everything else."

I rolled my eyes. "Those are just words. Your career is everything, and I get what's leftover. You're probably headed back to LA tomorrow to do another sex scene with Mandy. I could throw up just thinking about it."

"That's where you're wrong. Mandy went back to rehab two weeks ago. Our story line was scrapped."

"What? I though she had an understudy."

"She did. But, after everything that happened with you, I went to the producers and suggested they kill me off. And they agreed."

"Wait. You asked them to kill you off the show that made you a household name?"

"Yeah. I hated the story line with Mandy's character. It was all a ratings ploy. But more importantly, after you left, all I could think about was a way to get you back. I get it now. I love acting, but I hate being a hired gun and having no control."

I smiled at the notion he didn't like having any control. He caught me. "You think that's funny, don't you?"

I shrugged. "A little."

"Then I hope you will keep listening with an open mind, because I have a plan, and it finally came together."

"Can I ask you something first?"

He brushed my cheek with the back of his hand. "Of course, my sweet girl. You can ask me anything."

His simple touch caused my body to flush. I exhaled. "If you are so hell-bent on getting me back, why did you let go?"

He hung his head. "Because you were right about so many things. My career caused you so much pain. The choices I made hurt you. The way you looked at me that day, I thought you were better off without me in your life."

I mumbled, "Then why are you here now? I haven't even heard from you. I thought you forgot about me."

"Nothing could be further from the truth. I knew I couldn't come to you until everything was solid. And now it is."

With my eyes downcast, I clutched my hands together. Should I let myself believe in us again? He reached over and tipped my chin to meet his gaze and the butterflies in my tummy took flight. "Keep your eyes on mine, angel. Everything has changed. I promise you. For starters, I have a new team."

That got my attention. "You do?"

"Yes. I fired the old team, and I've set strict boundaries for the new one. It seemed like I was working for them, instead of the other way around. Also, *First Bite* is killing me off in the third episode. I wrap right before Thanksgiving."

As a fan, I was outraged. "The third episode? How will the show survive without you? You're Drake Braden, *the* vampire, the one everyone tunes in for."

He grinned. "You realize you just became a total fangirl right before my eyes."

"Well, it's true. I hope you didn't ask them to kill you off because of me. I don't want you to stop doing what you love. It's everything that comes with it, that I can't live with."

"I didn't do it for you. I did it for us. Plus, the show isn't getting picked up for a seventh season anyway."

"It's not?"

"No. It's time for all of us to move on and pursue other projects."

"But don't you see, that's what I'm talking about. Your other projects. You could be shooting a movie in Russia for six months and another actress will throw herself at you and I'll be right back here, in this same horrible place."

"You won't. Remember all those meetings I had with Martin this summer?"

"Yes."

"The deal came through. My dad and I are producing a new show together. *The Alec Stone Chronicles.*

"Isn't that the book series based in Vegas about the undercover detective?"

"That's the one. You're looking at Alec Stone. The Network that produces *First Bite* picked us up for two years, ten episodes a year. And, the best part is, we shoot right here in Vegas. Not just exteriors, but everything. I made it part of the deal."

My walls cracked a sliver and my heart began to hope, just a little. "You'll be in Vegas?"

"Yes, sweetie. And before you give another thought to an actress throwing herself at me, I'm in charge of casting. I've already cast my costar. It's Madison from *First Bite*.

The sliver splintered even more. "Madison, I like."

"I know you do, and she's perfect for the part. In

fact, because of her, the network gave us a sweetheart deal. Dad can't believe I pulled it off."

The way his eyes sparkled about this new project drew me in further. He did this for us. I was so proud of him. "You're an amazing man. You can do anything."

He knelt down on both knees, reached in his pocket and fished out my engagement ring. "I can't do anything without you by my side."

I gasped. "But Derek...I'm..."

"I know, sweetie. You're scared. And that's okay. I'm brave enough for both of us. And I know you lost faith, but I have more faith than you can imagine. And if you don't feel strong, then know I will be here stronger than ever. You just have to believe in us, just a little. I'll do everything else. I'll spend the rest of my life doing nothing but loving you. Can you? Can you believe in us again?"

Tears pricked my eyes and my heart bloomed open. "Yes, I believe. I believe."

He offered me his hand, and I clasped it as if it was a lifeline, because it was *my lifeline*.

Derek cradled me on his lap. "I love you. God, I love you."

With his arms wrapped around me, I wept. "I love you too. Please, no matter what I do. Please don't ever let go again."

"Never. Never again. It's you and me, forever."

I dried my tears and looked into his watery eyes. He held up the ring and I nodded. Derek slipped it on my finger and said, "You are mine, and I am yours."

"We belong together."

His lips lightly touched mine. "Now and always."

He picked me up and headed toward the door.

"Where are we going?"

"We're going home, baby. I'm taking you home."

* * * *

We were back, back in our bed—our bubble. Derek was on top of me, filling me. These past weeks, my body felt like an empty vessel without him inside me. We melded into one another and he rocked me slow and gentle. His mouth came down on mine and our tongues mingled together. How I missed the way he tasted. When he broke our kiss, he peered deep into my eyes. I saw such raw love beaming from him. My emotions overpowered me and tears spilled down my cheeks.

He gathered me to him and held me. "Hey, please don't cry. What is it, angel? Are you feeling scared?"

I peeked up at him. "No, I'm not scared. I'm more in love with you than I ever thought possible. I want you to take me. Make us come—together. I give myself to you."

There was the look, my look. "That's my good girl. Just hang onto me. I've got you."

Derek took me, submerging me fully. He slid tight against my inner walls, reaching my most intimate center. I was more committed to him, to us than ever.

The way he held me and glided inside me with care catapulted our searing connection.

He caressed my face, and his lips met mine with passionate, tender kisses that set off a fluttering thrill in my belly.

"Sweetie, I missed you. I missed everything about you."

I grasped his broad shoulders and held on while he amped up his sensual thrusts. "I missed you too. Ah, oh God."

That smile, his smile, the one that was wicked mixed with sweetness spread across his gorgeous face. "I feel it, you're close."

He pressed his forehead to mine and our eyes locked on one another. Derek took control. His bounty of supreme strokes heralded us to the brink, and tossed us into orbit. We shuddered and shook, giving into our sublime release that sealed us together from this day forward.

Then the doorbell rang. *What the fuck!*

Derek grinned. "Perfect timing." He eased me on my back and pulled out.

"I was thinking, worst timing ever. Who is it?"

"It's Grimaldi's. Plan A was getting you back, and Plan B is putting some weight back on you."

"Well, that didn't take long."

Derek pulled on some shorts. "What didn't take long?"

I giggled. "Bossy Derek is back and ready to take

action."

He clasped my chin. "When it comes to taking care of you, I will. No arguments."

I grinned. "No arguments, Mr. Pierce."

His lips touched my forehead. "Good girl. I'll be right back. We'll have a little pizza picnic in the bed."

As Derek took off, I reveled in sheer joy. He was going to be my husband. He was my forever.

While he was downstairs gathering the essentials for our pizza picnic, I threw on my robe and padded out onto the balcony. A little chill had crept into the air for the first time—fall was on the way.

I tilted my head to the sky in search of my star. The Almach illuminated the evening sky like never before. It was a sign, a sign from my mom and dad that Derek and I truly belonged together. I closed my eyes in prayer.

Before long, I felt Derek's arms curve around my waist. "Hey, did you come out here to find your star?"

I pointed to the shining cluster. "Yes, it's right there."

"It's beautiful, just like you, my angel."

He turned me around and swept me into his arms. "So, tomorrow, I'm hoping you don't have to work. My wheels have been turning and I've made some tentative plans."

Intrigued, I peered up at him. "What kind of plans?"

He played with my hair. "Well, for starters, I want

to take you shopping for something special. I can't wait to start spoiling you again."

"I don't need to be spoiled, I just need you."

"I know, but this can't wait. Can we do it first thing in the morning?"

"Sure. I'll have to put in an appearance at the office in the afternoon. Is that okay?"

"It's excellent. It will give me a chance to prepare for tomorrow night."

"You're not going to tell me what's going on, are you? You're going to spring two things on me?"

"Would I dare spring anything on you?"

"Uh…duh… Of course you would. You're Jerry Springer."

He threw his head back and laughed. "Okay, you've made your point. I will tell you this. Tomorrow morning I'm taking you to pick out something special, and tomorrow night I'm doing something for you here. Which reminds me, we also need to pick up Molly from Brooke's first thing in the morning. I want both of my girls at home, our home."

"I want that too."

His mouth landed on mine and our lips merged together with a newly discovered devotion. His kisses were as glorious as my shimmering star.

Derek exhaled and gazed deep into my eyes. "You and Molly, you're my family. You're my everything."

Chapter Four

"Hi, I'm Marshall, welcome to Marshall Morris Florist. How can I help— Oh my God, it's you!" Julia and Brooke's friend, Marshall, had the patented deer in the headlights stare that Derek was accustomed to. His round face flushed beet-red, and I swore the buttons on his shirt nearly popped right off.

Derek offered his hand. "Hi, I'm Derek Pierce."

Marshall clumsily shook it. "Well, of course you are, silly goose. I know that. The question is, what are you and this delightful young lady doing here?"

Derek draped his arm around my shoulder. "I want my fiancée, Nia, to have a look around and find her favorite flower. She should always be surrounded by something as beautiful as her."

Marshall and I swooned a tad. What a romantic gesture. After the white hydrangeas ended up smashed on Derek's kitchen floor in LA, they were no longer an option for my wedding bouquet, or anything else. Yes, we were making a fresh start. We were finding our way back.

"Nia? You mean Brooke and Julia's friend Nia?"

"Yes. It's so nice to finally meet you."

"You too. And aren't you the lucky one. I've never heard of anything so enchanting as a man bringing his fiancée to a flower shop to pick out her favorite flower. You don't happen to have a spare gay brother lying around, do you?"

Derek chuckled. "I'm afraid not. Just a sister in Chicago. Sweetie, what do you think? Is anything jumping out at you."

"Do you like roses, Nia?" Marshall asked.

I wandered about the store. "Um…they're okay. I was thinking of another flower, but I can't remember the name."

Then I spied it. It was an exquisite display. A heavy cut-glass vase sat atop a dark cherry wood pillar-shaped table. It would be perfect in our entryway. I wasn't an expert like Julia, so I didn't know the name of the flowers in the vase, but it was exactly what I was looking for. They were open and sturdy with a burst of pinkish red springing forth.

"Marshall, what kind of flower is this?"

"It's a Stargazer lily. It's one of my all-time favorites."

I gasped. "Did you say Stargazer?"

"Yes. Do you like it? I think it's an excellent choice."

Tears sprang to my eyes. "I do. I absolutely love it."

Derek's hand entwined with mine. "Hey, what's with the tears?"

"My mom's middle name was Lily and I have my star, so it's perfect. Marshall your display is amazing."

Derek cloaked me in his arms. "Marshall, we'll take everything. The table, vase, and the flowers. I want to set up a regular delivery so Nia will always have fresh flowers."

Marshall was just as emotional as I was. "Oh, you two kids are going to have me bawling like a baby. I can already see it. Tonight I'll be watching *The Notebook* and eating a pint of Ben and Jerry's Cherry Garcia."

* * * *

"Reunited and it feels so good." Shannon bopped into my office singing a sappy love song. "I heard the news. I'm so glad you and Derek are back together."

I beamed. "Thank you. I guess I have to officially forgive you for calling him when my stepmother was here. You really had my back. I appreciate it."

"Anytime, boss. You can count on me."

"I almost forgot. Where were you last night? I thought you would be part of my Derek ambush."

A sheepish grin crossed Shannon's face. "Do you really want to know?"

"Well, you seem to really want to tell me, so go for it."

She sat down and leaned forward as if she had a juicy secret. "Last night, Walter and I had a three-way with Christa."

Why do people fucking tell me things? "You did?

Wow…I did not see that coming."

Shannon laughed. "We were all coming."

I put my hands to my face and willed my ears to fall off. "Oh my God. Did you like it?"

"I didn't think I would at first. Christa mentioned it to Walter during spin and then he asked me. I mean, I didn't want him to do her without me…"

"So you figured, if you can't beat 'em, join 'em?"

"Something like that. Have you ever done one?"

"No. I don't think I would like it. Isn't it confusing? Here's a nipple, oh look a ball. Where do you focus?"

She howled with laughter. "Well actually…"

"You so do not have to tell me."

Not only didn't I want any free balling, titty rubbing details, I wasn't about to share my Christa kiss. Oddly enough, Shannon said she thought this might bring her and Walter closer together. If it worked for them then awesome. I only had one man on my mind. I couldn't wait to get home to him for the second part of my Jerry Springer surprise.

Jake arrived to pick me up. I texted Derek I was on the way.

He texted back. "Perfect. You have a massage appointment with Sven."

Ah crap! Who the hell is Sven? I didn't like massages. It was too difficult for me to relax. I texted back a tirade of why this wasn't a good idea, but then I deleted it. I should trust him. Just what did this Sven have in store for me?

* * * *

Derek stood before me in our bedroom wearing nothing but a purple silk tie, a hand towel draped over his arm, and a wicked smirk. "Hello, I'm Sven. I'm going to be your masseuse."

What a relief, and a delectable sight! This was exactly what we needed—a fun evening of playing. I was in, a hundred percent.

"Why, Sven, what would my fiancé say?"

"He's the one who booked the appointment."

Molly ran into the room and jumped on the bed. It was covered with extra sheets and a stack of fluffy towels rested at the foot of the bed.

We chuckled and then Derek returned to Sven mode. "This is my furry assistant." He promptly picked up a dog toy, chucked it down the hall, and shut the door. "Now, where were we, Miss Kelly? Ah, yes if you would kindly disrobe."

I stripped down to my panties, while a pulsing warmth flared through me.

He tugged on my thong. "These will only get destroyed. I want you naked. I insist."

He slid my panties off and motioned for me to lie down. "On your back, please."

As I reclined on the bed, I spotted Jasmine Vanilla massage oil, a feather tickler, and a bottle of lube.

He put down the hand towel and slipped off his necktie. "Your wrists, Miss Kelly."

I obliged and he bound them together and swiftly fastened them to the bed.

I pulled on my restraints. "Don't I get to touch you, Sven?"

He slid his fingertips along my jawline. "Hmm... touching costs extra."

It made me want to touch him more. Being tied up only fueled my arousal. It took me to a heady fuck space, where I could forget about everything, but how wet he made me. I wriggled on the bed and spread my legs.

"Sven" opened them even wider. "Mr. Pierce told me what a greedy little thing you are. You should know I charge by the orgasm."

"Oh, but I'm such a naughty girl. I don't have any money to pay you."

He knelt on the bed between my legs. "We'll have to take it out in trade. Now, let's see how wet you are."

Two fingers dipped inside and I gasped. My slit was already drenched. Taking matters into my own hands, I bucked on those fingers, forcing them deeper into my sweltering need. I rode on them at a rigorous pace as the sturdy digits grazed my hot spot. I amped up my efforts, craving a quick release.

"Look what a bad girl you are. You need to be reminded who's in charge, Miss Kelly." He removed his fingers, picked up my legs, and secured my knees to my chest. "You will be punished for that deviant display."

His spankings landed one right after another, on my taint, my cheeks, my sinful, slick cunt. All the blood rushed to my disorderly pussy. My impatient orgasm fizzled and spiked. I wailed, and without control shot forth a jet stream of juices. "Oh fuck, I can't help it. I'm sorry, Derek, ah…I mean Sven."

With that, we cracked up laughing. "Sven" grabbed a towel and dried my wetness. He placed another dry towel under me. "I might have to charge you double for that orgasm."

"You can put it on my tab. I plan on racking up quite a bill."

His hand clasped my chin and he stared deep into my eyes. "Who's in charge of that beautiful pussy?"

His commanding tone sent a spiraling gooeyness firing through my belly. In an attempt to steady my erratic heartbeat, I exhaled. "You are. You're in charge. My body belongs to you."

The corners of his mouth rose. "Good girl. Now, relax and let me take care of you."

My body grew jelly limbed and sank into the mattress. "Sven" rubbed oil on his hands and went to work on the arches of my feet, which were sorely in need of relief. His sexy hands were sublime. He touched all the right pressure points in just the right way. My fiancé was an evil genius.

The front of my body was free of tension and yet

tingling from his touch. He released me from my restraint and rubbed my wrists.

Keeping up our charade I asked, "So, Sven, what's your last name?"

He cleared his throat. "Um…it's uh Smorgesbord."

I giggled. "Sven Smorgesbord. Where did you go to school?"

"Uh…I went to the University of Toaster Strudel."

We chuckled and I added, "Oh, Toaster Strudel, a fine massage school and tasty breakfast treat."

His lips graced mine with a sweet kiss, and then Derek gave me that look. "Turn over. There's a perfect little bottom that needs tending to."

"I would hate to argue with you, Sven, but my bottom was sufficiently spanked."

"That does sound like an argument. Just what will I do to that gorgeous ass?"

I flipped over in a hot second. I couldn't wait. My body boiled and craved more.

First, "Sven" delighted me with a sensual shoulder massage. Every ounce of stress and strain fell away. He picked up the feather tickler and ran it down my spine. I released a series of contented moans and whimpers. The tickler sent tiny flickers flashing within, increasing the moisture dripping down my inner thighs. Then, he arrived at my ass. The man's obsession of my curved posterior never wavered. It was his favorite plaything. It was his.

He traced the feather over my cheeks and down the

middle of my crack. I squirmed and opened my legs. He teased my taint and floated the feathery fun wand down the backs of my legs.

His voice possessed that husky tone. The one that said he was bone-hard. "Lift your hips for me. I'm going to tend to your ass, but first I have to taste you."

I happily did what I was told. He tickled my sex with the feathers and blew lightly, igniting rippling sensations roaring through me. Then he gripped my hips and buried his face in my saturated pussy, helping himself to a generous mouthful. His hands held me in place while he ate me out from behind.

His fingers dove inside with an array of tantalizing thrusts. "I'm going to take you to the edge, and hold you there. Don't come until I tell you to."

I shrieked in pleasure, thinking I said okay, but who the fuck knew? The tip of his tongue flicked over my clit and then delved inside me, replacing his fingers. He tightened his grip on my hips and feasted on me with abandonment. His vehement suckling talents proved to be too much. From out of nowhere, a mighty surge of pressure built up and busted out of me like a rainstorm. *Oh shit!* I wasn't supposed to come yet. I cried out and expelled my disobedient juices. Derek released me and I face-planted on the bed in exhaustion.

I heaved. "I'm sorry. I didn't mean to. Are you mad?"

He drew me to him. "Come here. Of course I'm not mad. We're just playing. I mean, there was a reason I didn't want you to come yet. It was for your benefit, but I got as carried away as you did."

"I feel bad. You did all this for me, and I haven't done a thing for you. Your balls must be blue." I glanced down at Derek's raging hard-on in need of serious relief. The sight of it stirred me to my fiery center. "I'm always ready for more, Sven. Although, I have two orgasms on my tab, and I can't even give you a tip."

The most devilish grin appeared on his face. "Actually, I'm going to give you, the tip."

My eyes darted to the lube, then back to Derek. He caressed my face. "I think you're ready. I think we're ready."

I nodded in agreement and he swept me up into an all-consuming kiss that heated me from head to toe. Yes, I wanted this. I wanted to experience everything with Derek.

"I'm ready." I got on all fours on the side of the bed and offered myself to him.

"That's my good girl." He glided his hands over my cheeks in encouragement. "Just close your eyes and listen to my voice. Spread yourself for me, a little wider. That's it. I'm going to take you to the edge again. I want you to come for me, but not until I'm inside your ass. Understand?"

"I understand."

"If it's too much, just say the word, baby, and I'll pull out. And, Nia?"

"Yes?"

"I love you, sweet girl."

"I love you too."

"Let's get you relaxed."

His words alone worked me up. I was wetter than a fucking slip and slide. He surveyed my dewiness in appreciation. "Yes, my pussy is so ready." I percolated under his skillful hand stroking me to the edge. When my moans turned to groans, I heard the bottle of lube click open. Derek spread my cheeks, and placed a heaping dollop of lube on my tightest pucker. He also spread a thin sheen over my taint. "I've always said this was an untapped wonderland."

He skimmed his slippery fingers along my untapped wonderland. All those tiny nerve endings sparked, triggering more trickling juices. I desperately wanted to touch myself, but hadn't been given permission. My clit craved attention as a blaze burned inside me and emanated outward.

"I'm going to open you up with two fingers. Breathe for me."

Two gentle digits pried their way inside. *Oh fuck, yes!*

My body convulsed in delight. His fingers induced an onslaught of squishy squirts.

"That's it, my naughty girl. You love this. I need you to take a deep breath and touch yourself."

Yes! My hand rubbed my swollen clit with lightning speed. I expelled a huge breath. "Ah, Derek, please, I'm so close."

His tip touched the entrance of my snuggest opening. It squirreled its way inside and stilled while my body adjusted to the heavenly intruder. I released a lungful of air. Derek rocked his mighty crown inside, and I rubbed myself silly. This torrid sensation was pure pussy melting ecstasy.

I struggled to keep my orgasm at bay. "Ah God, Derek, yes!"

"Oh fuck. You feel amazing, baby. It's so tight. I can't hold on much longer."

I wanted him to come in my asshole, so it would belong to him too, but he pulled out and slid his massiveness up and down my tainted wonderland. His smooth, fluid cock flesh energized an outpouring of breathtaking spasms. They overtook me and my orgasm frantically broke free. Derek maximized the impact by pressing my ass cheeks together, surrounding his dick with a tight, slippery tunnel.

A loud groan tore from his throat and he spewed his hot creamy cum on my back. I collapsed on the bed in a heaping mass of aftershocks. *Holy hell!* That was crazy great.

Derek palmed my ass. "Be still, sweetie. I'll be right back."

Being still was all I could manage in my post Sven, tip-like state.

He returned with a warm washcloth and wiped me clean. "You were magnificent, my angel. There, all done. Can you roll over for me?"

I flopped my body right side up. "Just barely."

He hoisted me in his arms. "Come here, my sweet girl. I'm going to take care of you." My head nestled into the crook of his arm, and my spongy limbs grew heavy. "Baby, you're exhausted. We'll have a quick bath and I'll put you to bed right after we eat."

I mumbled, "I wanted to cook for you. I was going to make you Thanksgiving soup."

He kissed the top of my head. "I don't know what Thanksgiving soup is, but if you make it, I'll love it."

I prattled off my ingredients and nearly fell asleep somewhere between mushrooms and green beans.

Derek eased me into the tub. "I've taken care of dinner for tonight."

I perked up. "What? You cooked?"

He climbed in the tub and cuddled me from behind. "No, settle down. Julia did. She sent over fried chicken and mashed potatoes. We need to put a little weight on you."

"That ought to do it. Normally I'd argue with you, but you're right, and Julia's specialty is hard to resist."

"Thank you for not arguing with me. We'll mark that down as a first."

The aroma of my Jasmine Vanilla bodywash awakened me, bringing me back to my feisty self. "I didn't argue about the tip. Does this mean I'm no longer an ass virgin?"

He chuckled. "Well, not exactly. It was just the tip

and I didn't come inside you."

I angled my face to his. "I wanted you to."

"You did?"

I grinned. "I did. And, I wanted more. You may have turned me into a dude. All I'm going to think about is butt sex."

He gave me his glorious, sexy smile. "I love it. I'm going to marry one kinky lady."

"You are. There's something about playing. The minute you tied me up and took charge, it took me to another dimension. I felt even more connected to you and free, like I didn't have a care in the world. I want to experience everything, like the riding crop and nipple clamps and cum in my ass."

"Really? If you insist."

"I insist."

He drew his mouth to mine for a peck. "You never cease to amaze me. The way you've entrusted your body to me, I plan on taking good care of it for the rest of my life."

"That is an excellent plan, Mr. Pierce."

Chapter Five

Two days later, we received the dreaded call. Larry Wall was out of jail. He was still on probation and couldn't leave the state of California, but that didn't quell the look of worry in Derek's eyes when he told me.

Jake drove me to the club that day and escorted me to my office. Usually he was free while I worked, but now he was stationed right outside the entrance in the car.

Shannon noticed, so I confided in her about Larry. I went to my office, and before I could call Julia, my phone blew up. Wow. Telling Shannon was like telling everyone. I should be more careful. The never-ending barrage of vibrations reverted me back to old habits. I ignored the phone and left it on my desk while I taught my private class.

I worked myself harder than ever. The sweat poured out of me like a river. Luckily, I kept a change of clothes in my locker. I took a quick shower and donned a fresh outfit.

As I headed back to my office, my very own angry villagers stood before me. Derek, Julia, Brooke, and Lacey equipped with crossed arms and pissy faces. What did I do?

Julia led the brigade. "Nia, where's your phone? We've all been worried sick."

"It's in my office. I don't get what the big deal is. Jake is right outside the door."

Derek shook his head. "I thought we were clear about the phone, especially now."

"I'm sorry. I didn't mean to worry all of you. The phone wouldn't stop buzzing and I freaked out for a minute." I spotted Shannon shifting sheepishly behind the group. "Shannon, you should've let me break the news about Larry in my own time."

"I'm sorry if I overstepped. I've never even laid eyes on Larry Wall and I'm scared. I'm scared for you."

Derek jumped to her defense. "This isn't about Shannon. I'm glad she called everyone, because they needed to know. It doesn't matter how they found out. The real issue is you and your phone. Ladies, I need a moment alone with Nia."

Oh, fuck he called me Nia. The girls hugged me before taking off. I peered into Derek's angry eyes. I was in for it.

His voice was steely and quiet. "In your office. Now."

Once inside he picked up my phone. "Do you realize you left this unlocked? And the door was hanging wide open? This is unacceptable."

"I'm sorry. It won't happen again."

"Shut the door."

I pulled the door closed. "Derek, I said it won't

happen again, what more do you want?"

"You know what I want. I want you to finally get it. I want you to take your safety as seriously as I do. And I want you to get over your hang-up about the fucking phone."

"Okay. I get it. I won't leave the phone unlocked or out of my sight. I promise. It's just that the minute I left you this morning, I felt anxious. And when I got here, I needed two minutes to breathe, and then my phone went crazy."

"Nia, it went crazy because your friends love you. They're concerned. Remember the day after Julia's miscarriage. You called her to make sure it was okay to come over. How would you have felt if she didn't answer the phone?"

"I never thought about it like that."

"With Larry out of jail, things are going to be stressful enough. Please, sweetie, just answer your phone and keep it with you. You have to protect yourself and our privacy."

"You called me sweetie. Does that mean you're not angry with me anymore?"

He sighed. "It means I can't stay angry at you. I love you too much. Come here." His protective arms folded around me. They were my security, my solitude.

* * * *

"Marshall, what service. Come on in." That

evening, Marshall Morris, the florist, dropped by personally with my table, vase, and Stargazer lilies. Julia and Brooke were right. He really was the best.

"I could've had my delivery boy come, but I decided you needed my personal attention."

Surely, it had nothing to do with stealing another peek at Derek?

"I was thinking of putting the table right here by the staircase."

"Oh, it's perfect. No direct sunlight. That's what these lilies need." He put the table in its prime spot and placed the vase on top with a thud. "This is a little heavy, hun. If you and Derek get into a tiff and you're looking for something to throw, pick something else. Or better yet, just throw *me* at him."

I giggled. "I will keep that in mind."

"Now, if you want your lilies to last two weeks, I have little tricks I can show you."

"That would be great. I was just getting ready to pour a glass of wine. Would you like one?"

"Well, aren't you the sweetest. You twisted my arm."

"Come on back to the kitchen and bring the flowers."

We arrived in the kitchen and Marshall's eyes wandered about. "So, is...uh..."

"Derek here? Yes, he's outside with our dog, Molly."

"I love dogs. I have a Maltese named Kailani." He

whipped out his phone and showed me his cute, tiny white pooch. "She's so little, you could put her in your pocket."

"She's precious. Molly isn't so little anymore. She's eight months old and growing."

Marshall showed me how to cut the lilies and remove the pollen buds. He grew a little quiet while we sipped the wine.

"Is the wine okay, Marshall? We have red if you'd rather have that?"

"The wine is great. I was just wondering about the... It's none of my business...but there is a man in a black car outside your house."

"That's Jake. He's my...driver. It's all good."

"Good. I have a confession to make. I know about what happened to you and Derek in April, with your estranged husband. I also knew Larry Wall."

It was as if Marshall knocked me on the head with that vase. "How did you know him?"

"He had a standard order at the shop. He'd always buy two dozen red roses, but we always sent them to different women. One time I goofed and sent the roses to the wrong woman and he came in personally to let me have it. I thought he was going to pop me one. I heard he got out of jail. I'm sorry."

"I am too. I also think I'm going to need more wine. How about you?"

"Oh, hun, just keep this glass full. Let me get these flowers in water for you."

I poured the wine and checked on my Thanksgiving soup. Last year, when I made Thanksgiving dinner at Julia's, I took all the leftovers and threw them in a pot. It was the best soup I ever made. I improvised after that with white meat turkey breast, low sodium turkey stock, green beans, and mushrooms. Then I took a couple sweet potatoes, softened them a bit in the microwave and put them in the food processor with onions, carrots, garlic, and celery. It was a hit.

Voices booming at the front door made me jump, until I heard uproarious laughter. Sammy and Coco led the way. They gave me a quick sniff and lick, and trotted outside to play with Derek and Molly. Marshall escorted Julia, Phillip, and Brooke to the kitchen. They came bearing casserole dishes and booze. I barely had a chance to greet them when the doorbell rang again. Marshall hopped to like a jolly butler. Lacey and the Petersons arrived.

Sue held up her environmentally friendly grocery bag. "Nia, I believe I have your favorites." She delighted me with brie, havarti, soft white cheddar, gouda, and fresh mozzarella. It was like crack for cheese addicts.

I hugged her. "Thank you. Really, thank all of you for coming and bringing food. It means a lot to me, to us."

"Hey, Nia, any chance a certain someone could take a break and join us?" Lacey asked.

"Of course. Go get Jake. Is anyone else coming? I'll get the plates."

Lacey scrunched her face. "Well, I asked Christa, but she said she already had plans with Walter and Shannon. Why anyone would volunteer to hang out with Walter is beyond me."

Oh God, another episode of "Four Boobies and a Fuck Stick" was about to stream live on the Walter James porn network. No wonder he possessed an extra lilt in his step these days. What a scam artist. "Let me fuck this other chick. It will bring us closer." I hope Shannon knew what she was doing.

Jeff checked his phone. "I just got a text from Nancy's husband, Kevin. 'The girls hit happy hour early and we're not going to be able to make it.'"

"Well, that's too bad, because this is the place to be," Sue added.

Brooke glanced up from her phone. "Tom sends his love, and wishes he could be here."

"When's he getting back?" Phillip asked.

"Just in time for our engagement party. Which reminds me, it's on Halloween at the club, and costumes are mandatory."

Marshall swigged his wine. "Oh, Brooke, am I invited too?"

"Of course. I was going to ask you to do some arrangements."

"Perfect. I can see it now. Derek and I can dress up as Butch Cassidy and the Sundance Kid."

On cue, Derek walked into the kitchen. He cocked his head as if to say, "Where did everyone come from?"

I smiled and shrugged. Earlier, I teased him about needing a little riding crop discipline. I suppose Butch Cassidy would have to wait to tan my hide.

Lacey returned with Jake. Marshall's head whipped back and forth between Jake and Derek. Clearly, he wanted to be the meat in the middle of a Jake and Derek sandwich. Did everyone have three-ways on the brain?

"Where are the dogs?" Julia asked.

"They're lying on the grass. Molly wore them out." Derek replied.

With that, we all grabbed a plate and sat down to our eclectic buffet. We had Thanksgiving soup, Sue's spicy chicken salad, Brooke's broccoli and brown rice, and Julia's chili. The table grew quiet while everyone tucked into their food.

Marshall broke the silence. "This is quite a smorgasbord."

I nearly choked on my cheese. *Sven Smorgasbord.* Derek suppressed a chuckle, draped his arm around my shoulder, and whispered in my ear, "You're thinking about Sven, aren't you?"

I nodded with a devilish grin. He pressed his lips against my temple. "I'm thinking about the riding crop. Don't drink too much wine, young lady. I'm still going to take it to your bottom when everyone leaves."

I grabbed up my wineglass, emptied it in one gulp, and then handed it to him with a smirk. "More wine please."

"You're such a bad girl," Derek whispered as he rose to retrieve my wine. He trickled it slowly in my glass. "Just say when."

I teased. "Oh, fill it up."

"Oh my God!" Julia exclaimed. "You two never stop. Guys, we better eat fast before Derek and Nia do it on Brooke's broccoli and brown rice."

* * * *

"Derek, we are the worst hosts ever. Did you see how fast everyone ate and hit the road?" We were back in our bedroom. A tuckered out Molly relaxed on the bed. "Gee, poor Molly looks so comfy. I hate to disturb her. Maybe the riding crop will have to wait."

His animalistic gaze penetrated me. "Maybe you're going to strip down to your panties and wait for me by the loveseat facing the wall. Do it now, Nia."

My skin flushed and broke out in goose bumps all at once. I scurried to the armrest of the loveseat, overwhelmed with arousal as I rid myself of everything but my now wet thong.

My heart pounded while I heard Molly's collar jingle, followed by Derek shutting the door. He brushed my hair to one side and descended his lips along the curve of my neck. I quaked, and transported to that place, our place. He sealed our bodies together and his thick, rigid cock pressed into my spine.

Derek's nibbles on my shoulder made me squirm. I angled my face to his and he took possession of my mouth. Our tongues came together, but his was in charge. His hand captured the nape of my neck and he held me to him with a needy passion. It stole my breath and a wellspring of saturation spread below.

He released me and anchored my shoulders, so I faced the wall. His hot breath flowed over my skin. "Was somebody a bad girl tonight?"

I heaved. "Yes, I was a bad girl."

"Do you deserve to be punished?"

"Yes. I misbehaved, and my panties are wet."

His index finger ran over the thin cotton fabric. "What should I do about that?"

My pulse quickened. "Tear them off, please, tear them off."

He ripped them from my body. "Now bend over and close your eyes."

I obeyed with my ass in the air and the side of my face resting on the cushion. I heard the rustling of Derek's clothes hitting the floor and his feet padding over the carpet. He certainly took his time while I maintained my position, trembling in anxious longing. I was tempted to open my eyes. It was sheer torture waiting for him. The room grew silent. Did he leave? A misty sheen of wetness dripped down my inner thighs. My clit twitched in rich arousal. I allowed a daring hand to dive between my legs and graze over my soft slickness. It was a risky little move, but I took it. My naughty fingers wriggled my folds with gusto. Who knew how long I had to go at myself before—

—"Nia Kelly, you little fiend. You've just landed yourself in more trouble, young lady."

Well, fuck me, hard. I could only hope.

A dresser door opened and closed, and a thud followed. My eyes were still squeezed shut, but he was right behind me. I felt the heat radiating off his body.

He slipped the blindfold around my head. "I wasn't going to blindfold you, but you're very disobedient tonight. Take those mischievous hands and open yourself to me. Show me my naughty pussy."

My mouth went dry and beads of sweat prickled on my skin as I spread my cheeks and my most delicate tissues for him.

He placed his hand on top of mine and pulled me open wider. "There, that's better. Hold just like that."

His index finger ran the length of my badlands and sent a rousing shiver streaming through me. He repeated the same motion, skating the handle of the riding crop over my vibrating pussy flesh. He pushed the tip inside me and my inner muscles gripped it as it shifted back and forth. My lusty hole surged with a renewed deluge of juicy squirts.

I panted. "Oh yes, more. I need more."

He removed the great humping handle. "You think you deserve more after misbehaving?"

I whimpered, "Yes."

"You've made a mess on the riding crop." Derek

perched the handle at my lips. "Lick it clean."

I sucked my saturated tormentor inside. My taste buds were struck by the leathery texture of the crop and my sweet nectar. With the blindfold, I was cast further into another world where namaste met naughty play. Derek was pure fuck magic. I was so lost in my mouth task, my hands slipped from their spreading duties.

He retreated the handle. "So disobedient. I told you to leave your hands there. You'll have to be punished more severely."

He plucked up my wrists and slapped the furry handcuffs on them. The fur tickled the top of my crack. I was bound, blindfolded, and boiling with desire. Derek brushed the crop over my bottom and I braced for the first crack.

His voice was low and husky. "Baby, you need a safe word, in case it's too much. We're just playing. I don't want to hurt you."

"You won't. You never have. Please, Derek. I want it so bad."

"Safe word, my angel. No arguments. You're already in enough trouble."

My mind drew a blank, but my mouth blurted, "Wine!"

A sharp crack of the crop landed on my right cheek. It stung more than Derek's hand and produced a weightier buzz on my slit. His hand fondled the heated area. Another smack on my crack and left cheek followed.

Derek dove his fingers inside me to investigate the crop's effect. "You never fall short of amazing me, sweet girl. I love the way your body responds to its punishment. You're just such a fucking bad girl. You want more?"

"Yes. More."

A zealous barrage of swift swats ensued. My cunt gushed like a babbling brook, while my body amped up to glorious climax. I cried out in burning ecstasy, teetering between pain and pleasure. I was a flared-up fireball, ready to be tossed into space.

I heard the riding crop hit the floor and Derek palmed my burning cheeks. "You're so ready, baby. It's time to shower my hand, angel."

He worshiped my drenched slit with his hand, roaming over my fluttering cunt crease. I craved him inside me, but didn't dare ask. A swell of pressure reverberated within. Right before I fully let go he shunted me with his steely cock and catapulted me over the cliff of awesomeness. I screamed his name while he chastened me with dominate blows. His strokes quieted and he pulled out. Before I could protest, he freed my wrists and maneuvered me to him.

He ripped off my blindfold and I looked into those ice-blue eyes. He wore the grin of a delighted devil. His mouth seized mine with a fierce vengeance. His alluring tongue coiled about like a roving snake charmer. Hungry whimpers and groans permeated the air. My legs were so weak I could barely stand.

He released me and wrapped my hair around his hand. His commanding glare bore through me. "You're a very messy young lady. First the riding crop and now my cock."

I sunk to my knees. "Let me tidy you up."

He hissed. "That's a good girl."

I opened wide and lavished my mouth on his cock. My tongue polished his pole to an immaculate shine, relishing in my taste. I eased off and jacked him with my hand, producing a juicy morsel of pre-cum. I peeked up at him smiling in my triumph and guzzled him back into my earnest, wet mouth. I formed a tight suction and worked him even harder. My lips glided over every contour of his bulging veins. Then I sucked in a breath and his tip toyed with my tonsils.

Before I could consume a hearty throatful, he released my mouth. "Your punishment is over, sweet girl. Come."

He swept me up in his arms and carried me to the bed. I was on my back peering up at my beautiful fiancé. My eyes cascaded over his long, rippled build, from his broad shoulders to his protruding pecks, and that V-thing on his abs. Derek was absolute perfection standing before me. But his love for me—our love— surpassed it all. As he climbed on top and made love to me, he took my mind, body, and soul on a new journey. It was place of peace, a place of calm. It was home.

Chapter Six

"You've got to be kidding, Brooke." It was three days later. Brooke was in my office. She talked to Sonya again.

"For what it's worth, she sounded really sincere."

"Sincere about what?"

"About wanting to help you now that Larry's out of jail. Maybe she knows something that could keep you safe."

"So, let me get this straight. I'm supposed to believe that the woman who hated me and was in love with Larry Wall, all of sudden wants to help me. You do realize, despite everything, I bet she's still into him. Now that he's out of jail, she's probably using me as bait to lure him back."

"I don't think so. If anything, she wants to stick it to him for what he did to her. She's finally putting her life back together."

"Are you two like long lost friends? I had no idea you had such a soft spot for Sonya."

"Nia, you are my friend. My loyalty is to you, but I do feel bad for her after our talk."

"How long did you guys talk on the phone?"

Brooke averted my eyes. "Actually, I ran into her. She has a new job at Downtown Summerlin, and I bumped into her while I was shopping. She seemed so sad and desperate to talk, so we had coffee together."

I slumped back in my chair. "You went for coffee? I don't understand. Why? Why would you do that?"

"I know you don't want to hear this, but deep down Sonya isn't a bad person. She worked at the club for ten years and when I came on board as her boss five years ago, she was...nice. She made a mistake and was led down the wrong path by Larry. Now she wants to help you. I think you should hear her out. I'll be right by your side, and Derek can be there too. Don't you think it's worth a shot to at least listen to what she has to say?"

"No. Are you forgetting she took the key off your key ring, and unlocked the door to Julia's guesthouse while I was sleeping? I was a sitting duck. Her mistakes nearly got me killed. I don't know how you can forgive her, let alone sit down at the same table and have coffee."

Brooke relented. "You're right. I'm sorry. It was stupid of me to even suggest it. I guess it's a good thing she turned down my invitation."

"Your invitation to what?"

"Well, don't freak out, but she noticed my engagement ring. I got so excited talking about Tom that I invited her to our engagement party on Halloween."

I gasped in disbelief. "You what?"

"I'm sorry. My mouth got the best of me. Haven't

you ever blurted out something you wished you
hadn't?"

I sighed. "All the time."

"She's not coming. She said she had to work and
wouldn't feel right about it because of you."

"Well, that's a relief. Did you ask her how she got
through security the night she scared me?"

"No. You know, that's my bad. I should've asked
her, but we started talking about the members, like the
Petersons and what everyone was up to. I guess I
forgot." She rose from her chair. "Look, I promise I
will never mention Sonya's name again or take her
calls. I've always told you I've got your back and I
mean it."

I smiled. "Thank you."

"Hey, speaking of which, Tom and I are copying
you and Derek. We are asking all the guests to make a
donation to Sammy's Place instead of gifts."

I was so touched I leaped out of my chair to hug
her. "Thank you, that means everything."

Brooke broke our embrace. "And I mean what I
said about Sonya. I will never mention it again."

"It's all good. I know your heart was in the right
place."

A knock on the door diverted our attention.
Shannon appeared in the doorway sporting a huge grin.
"Can I come in?"

"Sure." I replied.

"Brooke, I'm so excited for your engagement party.

We just got our costumes. I'm going to be Catwoman. Walter is going to be Batman, and Christa is going as Bat Girl."

"Wow! What a threesome." Brooke said without realizing her pin-point accuracy.

"It was Walter's idea."

I crossed my arms in annoyance. "Shannon, I told you last week, Derek and I are going as Catwoman and Batman. We already have our costumes."

"I thought you said Superman and Wonder Woman."

"I could never pull off Wonder Woman. Everybody would wonder where her boobs went. Julia and Phillip are going as Wonder Woman and Superman."

"Oh, that's right, I forgot. I'm sorry, but we already have our costumes too."

Brooke intervened. "Girls, there can be two Catwomen and two Batmen. Haven't there already been like ten of them on-screen? There's over two hundred people coming. It'll be fine."

I huffed. "This coming from the girl who posted her costume on Facebook a month ago, so no one else would come as a blonde Red Riding Hood."

"Well, it is my engagement party. And, I've always wondered if blondes have more fun."

Shannon twirled her golden tresses. "Lately, they do."

Oh man! She was talking about her three-way lay. She must be enjoying herself. Her face flushed crimson as she sauntered to the door. "Nia, I'm sorry about the costume screw up, but I think we're all going to have a blast. I'm so excited."

After Shannon left I shrugged my shoulders. "I'm excited for your party too, even if there's going to be two Catwomen. One thing's for sure, your engagement bash will be way better than mine."

Brooke laughed. "Uh... Way!"

* * * *

"Well, do you want the bad news or the bizarre news?" Molly and I cuddled on the bed, while Derek unlocked my jewelry armoire before joining us.

"How about the bad news first."

"Brooke ran into Sonya. She still wants to talk to me."

Derek's body went rigid. "That is out of the question."

"No argument from me. Brooke is the one you need to talk to. She wanted me to talk to her. She even invited Sonya to her engagement party."

He jerked up in bed. "She what? Is she coming, because if she is, we'll have to cancel."

"No. She's not coming. It'll be fine."

"What was Brooke thinking?"

"I don't know. It's was kind of weird, but I think it's fine now."

He nestled back into our cuddle. "So, tell me the

bizarre news."

There was no easy way to tell him about Christa's kiss. It wasn't a big deal, but keeping it from him for longer than I already did weighed on me. "I kissed a girl."

"Did you like it?"

"No. I'm not Katy Perry. And to be accurate, she kissed me. I was floored by the experience."

"I think my head just exploded. When did this happen and who—"

I sighed. "It happened when we were broken up and it was Christa, the spin instructor…"

A huge smile split his face. "Oh, the curvy one."

I could see the devious wheels turning in his head. "Oh my God! You are so imagining us kissing right now. You're such a guy."

He caught himself mid-daydream. "No. I'm just surprised."

"She said she wanted to do a three-way with us."

His eyes bugged out of his head. "She did. Interesting."

I pummeled him with a pillow, and Molly joined in, grabbing the pillow with her teeth and shaking it. "Hey, Molly, whose side are you on?"

He tossed the pillow aside. "Settle down, slugger. I don't want to have a three-way with Christa or anyone else. I only want a two-way with you."

I pouted. "Is that one of these secret things that guys want, like butt sex? Did you ever?"

"Well..."

My mouth gaped open. "I knew it. You had a three-way. I'm marrying an orgy guy."

He cracked up. "You're not marrying an orgy guy. It was a fluke. It only happened once."

"You were with two girls?"

He gathered me to his lap with a grin. "Yes. I was in college, there was a party, I was drunk, and there were two of them. I mean, I wasn't going to say no."

I crinkled up my nose. "What was it like? Was it the ultimate fantasy?"

He tapped his fingertip to my nose. "You're my ultimate fantasy."

I groaned. "Oh come on. You have to say that. I can take it. I mean, when it happened I was probably still in Junior High."

His grip tightened on me. "Hmm... You're always ready to drop your panties for some discipline."

"Well, after that riding crop, it's like, once you go crop, you're ready to drop."

He chuckled. "You don't have to drop right now. I actually have a little surprise for you."

Derek patted my bottom and lifted me off him. "Well, actually it's two surprises."

"Wait a minute. Are they surprises or decoys? You never answered my question about the three-way."

He shook his head. "If I tell you, you promise to keep it a secret?"

"If there's one thing about me, I can keep a secret."

"Yes, that's true. When I told you that Eden and I were just friends, you kept that secret, and you kept Eden's secret too."

"Of course. I never told anyone she's gay. So, orgy guy, tell me about fantasy threesome come true."

He sighed. "I fell asleep."

I giggled. "You fell asleep? Like what, with a pussy on your face or your dick in a mouth."

"You think you're funny, don't you?"

"I really do. So, for real, you fell asleep?"

"Yes, and it's a secret. I was so drunk and once I had, you know, came, the party was over."

"Well, then, one of the girls didn't get her turn?"

"No. But that girl was so drunk, she thought she did. So, I still got bragging rights."

"That's sounds more like a two-way and I'll owe you one."

"I guess you're right. Now, would you like your surprise? It's what you would call a doozie."

"I love doozies. Go for it."

"First of all, I got a new lock put on your armoire. It only has one key, and I'm going to keep it in the nightstand." He opened up the cherry wood door wide. There was a small safe installed. He circled the dial about and it clicked open. "I want to keep some of your pieces in here. Take a peek inside."

I hopped off the bed and looked. My heart melted. "Is that the Rolex you got me the day we—?"

He touched a finger to my lips. "Yes. And since we

are starting over, there's something else." He plucked another velvet box from the safe and got on one knee. "Nia, I want you to marry me and take this ring as a sign of my renewed commitment to you. That we will be together now and always."

He flipped open the box and I gasped. "Derek, it's amazing. It's...oh my God. I know that ring. Is it from Cartier?"

"Yeah, how did you know?"

"Julia. Oh wow! She is going to crap her pants when she sees it. She's been dropping hints to Phillip about the Trinity Cartier ring with the pink, yellow, and white diamonds for a year."

He cocked his head. "Is it a problem? Do you not want it?"

"Heck no, Julia can suck it. Just don't tell her I said that. She'd kill me." I clasped my hands to his face and brought my lips to his for a kiss. "Thank you. We are now and always and for eternity. This is perfect."

He pulled me to his bended knee and slipped the ring on my finger. "You wear it well, my angel."

"I kind of do, don't I?" I giggled staring at its beauty. "I do feel bad. Everything you've given me is so exquisite, but most of it I'm afraid to wear, even my engagement ring. And I'm scared to death I'll lose my mom's ring, so I don't wear it either."

He picked me up and sat me on the edge of the bed. "I thought about that too. I don't like you walking around with a naked ring finger, so I got you something else."

He reached into the armoire and produced another Cartier box.

"Derek, what did you do?"

A gleam flashed in his eyes as he handed over the box and watched me open it. "This you'll wear everyday, no arguments."

I pried open the box to reveal the ring that was truly me. It was the Trinity collection's black and white ring—simple, without diamonds, but beautiful. "Oh I love it. And you're right, I can wear it everyday, even when I'm teaching." I sprang to my feet and flung my arms around his neck. "Now, I can't decide."

He arched his eyebrow. "Can't decide which one to wear?"

"No, I can't decide if I should argue with you and be punished, say it's too much, and be fucked, or just say thank you and then you'll make love to me."

"I'll make a deal with you. If you promise never to leave the house without one of my rings you can have, all of the above. I'll take you across my knee and spank your bottom. I'll take you from behind and fuck you. And I'll take you in my arms and make love to you."

"I promise!"

Chapter Seven

"That's the ring! The Cartier ring I've been hounding Phillip for. When did you get that?" Wonder Woman turned into sulking woman when she spied my new ring at Brooke's engagement party.

The ballroom at the country club morphed into a spooktacular graveyard. Brooke and Marshall designed the haunting theme. There was a fog machine and an eerie glow that surrounded the room.

"He gave it to me weeks ago and I haven't worn it yet, because I knew you wanted it."

Julia grabbed my hand and shoved it under Phillip's nose. "This is the ring I was talking about."

Phillip shook his head. "Derek, you're killing me, you know that."

Derek put his hand on his shoulder. "Sorry, friend. I had no idea."

To ease the ring of fire, I said, "Oh no, Batman and Superman are about to throw down. Julia, who would you put your money on?"

She snuggled into Phillip. "Superman of course. He has super powers. And Wonder Woman would kick Catwoman's ass."

I laughed. "Are you sure? Catwoman has claws, *and* she's scrappy."

Julia gripped her torpedo tits. "Scrappy is no match for these bad boys."

We all cracked up, and Phillip took her by the hand. "Come on Wonder Woman, let's dance."

They made their way to the crowded dance floor. There were so many costumed guests, I hadn't had a chance to say hi to Brooke and Tom. Derek and I huddled up to the bar and grabbed a drink. Out of the corner of my eye, I spied our villains, the Joker and the Riddler. It was Tim and Keith. I hadn't seen them since our engagement party months ago. Wow! Tim made an excellent Joker and Keith looked great too.

The closer they got to us they broke up in hysterics. What were they up to?

Keith doubled over and clutched my hand. "Oh, you wouldn't believe what just happened."

Tim couldn't contain himself. "We almost got beat up. Did you know there's another Batman and Catwoman here?"

"Yes." I explained, "There was a misunderstanding with my friend, Shannon and they got the same costumes."

"Well, now we know," Tim said. "We saw a Batman and Catwoman and thought it was you guys. So we decided to get into our villain characters and went up behind your friend. We pretended to capture her like a prisoner and said, 'Gotcha.' She jumped and Batman nearly decked us. When we realized our mistake, Keith goes, 'Oops, wrong pussy.' And we took off."

Derek and I howled with laughter, while I raised my glass. "Boys, the correct pussy is right here."

"Yeah, and it's been way too long. Come here, girl." Keith pulled me into a hug. "It's so good to see you. And can I just say, you are working that catsuit. Damn, you look fierce. I'm not into girls, but if I was, I'd be tapping that."

I twirled so they could check me out fully. I felt sexy as hell in this skintight sleek costume, complete with headpiece and tail. It was a good thing my hair was hidden under the kitty cap because I was also hotter than hell. My brunette hair would have been limp and lifeless.

It was Tim's turn to greet me with a warm embrace. "At the risk of getting decked by my second Batman, you do look hot."

Derek snaked a possessive arm around my waist. "She does. You look incredible."

I touched my lips to his with a sweet kiss and got lost in Derek's ice-blue eyes. "Thank you."

"It's a good thing we're moving here," Keith announced. "Something tells me these two will be home in less than an hour for trick or treats."

I snapped out of my blue-eyed trance. "Did you say you're moving here?"

Tim beamed. "Yes. Derek made me head of wardrobe for *The Alec Stone Chronicles*. This weekend we're going to start looking for a house, maybe something here at the country club."

"That's the best news ever!" I exclaimed. "I hope we'll be neighbors. Hey, you remember Steve and Scott from our engagement party? Their house is still for sale. It's right next to Julia's."

"That would be great. Do you know who their real estate agent is?" Keith asked.

I replied in a mocking tone, "It's Batman."

"I bet he'll make us an offer we can't refuse." Keith joked.

Derek said, "Speaking of which, our mirror image is headed this way."

"That's our cue, Riddler. Exit, stage left."

"Later, dynamic duo." Keith and Tim sidled into the thick of the party guests and disappeared.

There was still no sign of Brooke and Tom in the crowd. I was dying to see her in a blonde wig and Red Riding Hood ensemble. If it was hot in my catsuit, I can imagine Tom was roasting in his Big Bad Wolf costume.

Jake and Lacey were dressed as biker dude and chick. It was the only costume Lacey could talk him into. The four of us came to the party together, but I hadn't seen them since we arrived. Knowing Jake and Lacey, if the private dining room was unlocked, they were in there getting after it. That didn't sound like a bad idea.

Walter and Shannon landed in front of us. The Batmen exchanged an awkward greeting. Derek still didn't care for Walter, and it was difficult for me to maintain an even keel with him. Every time I grew more comfortable with him for Shannon's sake, he did something to erase his good standing. The latest eraser joined us at the bar. Christa filled out her Batgirl costume with great aplomb. If participating in three-ways was something Shannon really wanted; then God Bless. If she was doing it to hang onto Walter and ended up getting hurt then, not so much. When Derek spotted her, a knowing smirk danced on in his lips.

I whispered in his ear, "Stop thinking about her kissing me."

Without skipping a beat Derek said, "Christa, nice to meet you. I've heard so much about you."

She lit up in his presence. "It's great to finally meet you. Wow! How did we get so lucky? Two Batmen instead of one."

I could see her three-way wheels spinning. A rush of pink stained her cheeks while her eyes sauntered from Walter to Derek. I liked Christa, but if Batgirl desired my Batman in her Gotham City, she could fucking forget it.

I handed her a cocktail to cool her down. "Thanks, Nia. Oh wow! That's a beautiful ring."

"Thank you. Derek's been spoiling me rotten."

Shannon took a gander too. "Nia, that's amazing. Gosh, all of your rings are gorgeous. Derek you have great taste. She wore her Rolex to work the other day and my jaw hit the floor."

Derek sipped his wine. "Thank you. I do love

spoiling my girl."

Shannon glanced at Walter. "I wish someone would spoil me."

The uncomfortable silence from Walter made me nervous, and I blurted, "You're welcome to borrow anything you'd like, for a special occasion. I hardly get a chance to wear it."

Derek tugged my cat tail in a sign of disapproval. This conversation grew thornier by the moment, until the swashbuckling Marshall joined us in his Captain Hook costume.

"Yo-ho-ho and a bottle of rum. Let's make mine a Malibu rum and coke."

I squealed, "Marshall, you brought Kailani. Look at you. You're the cutest Peter Pan ever." Without asking, I plucked Marshall's Maltese from his arms and held her close. We all *ooh'd* and *ahh'd* over the sweet little white dog. "How old is she?"

"She'll be six in December," Marshall replied. "I've had her for two years. Can you believe this little princess was at the shelter? Her owner passed away suddenly, and no one stepped forward to take her. I saw her on a segment on the news and I rushed right down to the Humane Society. The rest is history."

Kailani squirmed in my arms so I handed her back to Marshall. "Well, she certainly hit the jackpot."

Walter patted Kailani's head. "All dogs deserve a good home."

"Have we met?" Marshall asked.

Walter extended his hand. "No. I'm Walter James, and this is my girlfriend, Shannon, and our friend, Christa."

Walter knew how to giveth and taketh away. On one the hand, he was sweet with Kailani, and the other hand, when he said Christa's name there was a lecherous quality to his voice.

Marshall shook his hand. "You seem very familiar. I just can't place it. Have you ever been in my shop, Marshall Morris Florist?"

"No. I don't believe so," Walter replied.

"Well, maybe when you're out of your Batman costume it will hit me. Wow! Two Batmen, two Catwomen, a Batgirl, and a Captain Hook. There's a dirty joke in there somewhere, and when I think of it, I'll send a tweet."

Shannon laughed. "Don't forget about Peter Pan. And where's Red Riding Hood and the Big Bad Wolf?"

Marshall waved his hook. "Oh, that reminds me. Nia, I was supposed to tell you Brooke was looking for you."

"She is? We've been looking for her. And by looking, I mean, we've been drinking at the bar. I thought she'd be easy to spot. You two are the only ones wearing a red cape."

"Her family is here from Chicago, and Tom's is here from Florida," Marshall said. "They are keeping her busy, but she wanted me to tell you that Sammy's Place will be thrilled. The money is pouring in for your charity."

I smiled and glanced up at Derek. "That's such good news. Hey, are you coming by tomorrow with more lilies?"

"Lilies?" Shannon asked.

"Yeah, Derek arranged for Marshall to come by every other week with fresh Stargazer lilies."

"Oh, that's right. Lacey told me. Derek, could you be any sweeter?"

"I know, right. Jewelry, flowers, and Batman. That's the whole package," Christa added.

Walter set his drink down. "If you'll excuse me. This Batman could use a little fresh air." He took off in long strides toward the exit.

"Um…we better head out too. Come on, Christa."

"I'm right behind you."

I bet Walter said that last night.

The girls deposited their drinks on the bar and hurried after Walter. It seemed his Batmobile was bruised by all the gushing over Derek.

After they left, Marshall asked, "How long have you known Walter?"

"Not long, why?" I responded.

"I know him from somewhere. Until, I figure it out, it will tie my brain up in knots."

I gasped. "Speaking of tying things up. Look."

Our mouths gaped open as Sue, Nancy, and Sharon entered the room with their husbands. *Holy S and M!* They all donned black leather outfits fit for a dominatrix and master. The way they glided into the room with ease and comfort made me curious. After all, Sue and the chorus girls did give me the filthiest gifts at my bridal shower.

"Can you believe their costumes?" I asked. "Those ladies look hot."

Marshall leaned in. "I don't think they're costumes. I don't like to gossip, but I heard there was a BDSM club not too far from here. Their body language tells me they've worn it before."

"Really? Is it rude if I go over and ask? I'm dying to know." I placed my drink on the bar.

Derek grabbed my hand. "It would be rude if you didn't dance with me to our song."

"Unforgettable" piped through the speakers. One look in Derek's eyes and I abandoned my quest for fetish facts.

"You kids go dance. I'll try to find Brooke and send her your way."

I barely heard what Marshall said, since Derek gave me his million-dollar smile, led me to the dance floor, and swept me away in his arms.

I peeked up at him. "Did you ask Brooke to play this song?"

"I did, Miss Kelly. It's not befitting for Halloween, but it's our song, from our very first dance."

"I remember it as if it were yesterday."

"I remember you wouldn't let me lead. You've come a long way, my sweet girl."

"We've come a long way. I'm so glad we're back together. I was miserable without you."

"Put it out of your mind, sweetie. We're solid. Nothing will ever come between us again."

"Hey, there you are!" Brooke and Tom swayed next to us. She looked adorable in her blonde wig and bright red cape. Tom had banished his Big Bad Wolf headpiece. His slick backed hair was an indication of how sweltering the costume was.

"You guys look so cute. Your party is a hit," I said.

Brooke laughed. "You have no idea. Our families are turning it up. Even my grandmother is drunk. Julia and Phillip are hanging out with them. I hope Julia doesn't try to go round for round with my cousins. She'll never make it."

"I just hope my Uncle Shelley can keep his hands to himself," Tom added. "He took one look at Julia and his eyes practically flew out of his head. I told him to behave and he said, 'I'm eighty-years-old and harmless, but horny.' He's a piece of work."

"I would love to meet them," I replied. "I'm not sure how much longer we're going to stay though. These costumes are fun, but hot. I'm dying under here."

"You two look amazing. Don't worry about us and our families. They're keeping me on my toes. Plus, one look at Derek and they'll all want a picture. You'll get stuck here all night. I just wanted to make sure Marshall told you we raised a lot of money for Sammy's Place."

"He did. Thank you so much."

"Have either of you seen Jake and Lacey?" Derek asked.

They both laughed, and Tom confessed, "Well, earlier we snuck into the private dining room."

Brooke interrupted, "Only Jake and Lacey beat us to it. They forgot to lock the door."

"I guess the Big Bad Wolf won't get to see what's in your basket."

"Tom!" Brooke blushed. "Anyway we better head back and check-in with the tipsy, the drunk, and the three sheets to the wind."

"Have fun. And congrats. Your party kicks our party's ass."

Brooke said over her shoulder, "Thanks. Oh, and if you two lovebirds go into the private dining room, just remember to lock the door."

They scurried off and I resumed my adoring gaze into Derek's eyes. "I do have fond memories of the private dining room. I believe I did some of my best cock sucking in that very room."

He had that look. "And now I'm about to do some of my best spanking in there."

The breath lodged in my throat. "Have I been a bad girl?"

His eyes brimmed with fire. "Yes. You told your friends they could borrow your jewelry whenever they wanted, without discussing it with me. You're going to be punished in the private dining room, and at home you'll strip naked for me. Your breasts will be devoured until you're ready for the nipple clamps."

Spanking and nipple clamps? *Happy fucking Halloween to me.*

Derek's hands floated down my back and they settled on the upper curve of my bottom, sending a spurt of flickering desire whirling through me.

"Well, then, let the discipline begin, Batman."

He tightened his grip and whispered in my ear, "Go to the private dining room and wait for me. Leave the door unlocked and bend over the table. And, Nia, don't turnaround until I tell you your spanking is over. Understand?"

"I understand, Mr. Pierce."

He patted my ass with a gleam in his eye and off I went. As I maneuvered past the crowd, my eyes searched the room, hoping no one spotted me rushing toward the private dining room. God, what if *First Bite* fans stopped Derek on his way to spank me? I could be bent over a table all night.

Just as Brooke said, the room was unlocked. The moon streamed through the window producing the perfect amount of light for our Halloween spank. It drew me in and I went toward the glowing orb to look for my star. The Almach and most of the other stars were barely visible in the nighttime haze. It was the appropriate sky for such a ghostly, ghoulish night.

An undetectable sound in the room caused my head to snap around and catch a faint glimpse of a red cape and lock of blonde hair. "Brooke. Brooke, wait." She vanished out the door leading to the kitchen. I set off after her until I saw them on the table—Stargazer lilies shredded to pieces. My shaky hands caressed the soft petals. *What the fuck?* Who would do this? My breath was shallow and a sudden fear paralyzed me. Another door slammed shut and panic ricocheted within me. In my frightful, immobile state, I clenched the lilies. Trepidation knotted in my throat until Derek's gloved Batman hands embraced mine.

I exhaled in relief and attempted to turn to him. He grasped me by the shoulders and forced me to bend over the table. One hand secured me into place, while the other roamed freely over my ass. Did he not notice the flowers? I had to tell him what happened.

In a barely audible whisper I said, "Please... don't... The flowers—"

The light flipped on. "Get the fuck away from her, now!" Derek commanded firmly from the doorway.

"Oh my God! Walter? Jesus!" I ran away from him and into Derek's protective arms.

He clutched me to him. "Baby, you're shaking. Did he hurt you?"

"No. I thought it was you. Something weird is going on."

"Look, I'm sorry," Walter said. "I thought Nia was Shannon. I told Shannon to meet me in here. It was an honest mistake."

"I think it would be best if you went and found Shannon," Derek stated bluntly.

"Fine," Walter replied and lurched out of the room.

"Nia, tell me. What's going on?"

I led him to the table and picked up the mutilated petals. "I found these. It's like someone knew I was coming in here and they knew about the Stargazer lilies. It's so strange. I was standing by the window looking for my star and I heard noise. When I turned I could've sworn I saw Brooke heading out the door that leads to the kitchen."

"Sweetie, you must've seen someone else. Brooke would never play a joke on you like that. Plus, you heard her. She went back to hang out with her family."

"You're right, but I saw the red cape and blonde wig, I mean, who else would it be? Oh no. Unless it was Sonya messing with me."

"Sonya? I don't follow."

"Brooke put the Red Riding Hood costume on her Facebook page. She didn't want anyone else to copy her. Sonya could've seen it and came here tonight in disguise. Brooke invited her, remember? I don't know. Maybe I'm grasping at straws... I just want to go home."

Derek held me close. "Of course, my angel. Let's get you home."

My voice quivered. "Derek...he touched me. Walter...touched me. I think he knew it was me. I can't be around him anymore. Even if Shannon is my friend. I feel violated."

He rubbed my back. "He will never bother you

again. I'll see to it. I'm sorry he did that to you. It's my fault. I should've been here. I got sidetracked by Jake and Lacey. I told him we'd be leaving soon if he wanted to get the car. They're waiting for us out front." He tipped my chin to meet his gaze. "I'll take care of everything. But first, I'm going to take care of you. Come."

* * * *

Derek peeled me out of the catsuit and turned on the shower. "I'm going to feed Molly, and I'll be right in to wash you. Then I'm putting you to bed."

My shoulders slouched in disappointment. "But I thought...I mean, you said something about nipple clamps."

He kissed my forehead. "We'll see. Maybe. If you're good. For now, just get in the shower for me, and wash this night away. I'll be right back."

I stepped in the hot shower and exhaled. Derek was right. I needed to scrub Walter off my body, and my brain. I rotated the showerhead to its highest flow level and grabbed my Jasmine Vanilla bodywash. I squirted it on my exfoliating scrubby and slathered it over my breasts. The sensual scent and extreme shower current invigorated me.

The evening's eerie turn started to fall away. I washed my hair and applied conditioner, wondering what was taking Derek so long. The bottle slipped out of my hands and when I bent over to pick it up, the jetting stream of water pelted my taint, awakening my wonderland with longing. I reached around and spread my cheeks wide, just as Derek instructed me when he used the riding crop. It kindled a flame smoldering deep within. *Do I dare? I dared.* I lathered up two fingers and guided them into my anus. I reamed my tight tunnel and imagined Derek taking me there fully to his balls. If I could open my ass for him a little more, it wouldn't be much longer before he could have all of me, completely. I was lost in the thought of Derek claiming me wholly, for him alone.

"Nia!" Derek's voice echoed.

He startled me. I screamed and slipped forward. Derek caught me around the waist before I banged my head into the shower wall. He angled me to him with hooded seduction in his eyes. "Young lady, what did I walk in on? Were you pleasuring yourself without me?"

I swallowed hard. "I was just trying to… I dropped the bottle of conditioner and when I bent over, it just sort of happened."

His gaze remained firm and fixed. "Rinse out the conditioner."

I hesitated, and his voice grew more insistent. "Nia, do it."

I closed my eyes and stuck my head under the nozzle. When my task was complete, I opened my eyes and they raked over Derek's hulking, magnificent build. His ironclad cock enjoyed my misbehaving fingers as much as I did.

He crushed my breasts against the hardness of his chest. "Go dry off and bring me the belt on your robe."

With zero hesitation, I popped out of the shower and dried myself with the speed of a panther. I grabbed up my belt and presented it to Derek at the shower.

He cracked the door open. The corners of his mouth upturned with a dash of amusement, but his eyes inhabited a dark fiery heat. "Give me your wrists." He bound them together with a flourish. "I want you naked on the bed, flat on your stomach. While I finish my shower, think about how many times I should spank you for pleasuring yourself. I'm taking you across my knee, Nia. You've been a bad girl. Now, go."

I scampered to the bed and reclined on my tummy, so fucking glad I dropped the bottle of conditioner. While I waited for Derek, my mind and body coasted to our bubble of tranquility, where I was protected, loved, and super horny.

Exactly how many times should he spank me? The forthcoming swats on my bottom launched a dribbling leak from my saucy cunt. My ass relished Derek's large disciplining hand punishing it until it blistered in ecstasy. Riding the wave between pain and pleasure paid out in major dividends for my pussy. A little risk reaped high rewards for my blue-chip lady parts.

The sound of Derek's feet scuffing across the carpet caused that familiar dizzying in my stomach.

"Nia, spread your legs. Show yourself to me."

I opened up my thighs and trembled as his fingertips hedged along my weeping slit. "Hmm… you're drenched. I'm starting to think you're rebelling on purpose. Just the thought of going over my knee makes you wet."

I panted. "Ah…yes. I need to be taught a lesson."

"You most certainly do. How many times should I spank you?"

I blurted out proudly, "I was very bad. Twenty."

He removed his hand and kissed each cheek. "Twenty it is. Stand by the side of the bed."

I darted off the bed with volatility, flushed and primed for my allotment of spanks. With legs draped on the side of the bed, Derek's lap provided a wealth of opportunity. My tawdry behavior would reward me with rich orgasmic liquidation. The gleam in his eye as he guided me over his knee sent the blood surging from my fingertips to my toes.

His hands palmed my lush, expectant cheeks. "You do need to be taught a lesson. No more holding back. You've earned the spanking of your life, for pleasuring yourself in the shower. Do you remember your safe word?"

I murmured. "Yes. It's wine."

"You might need it."

The breath froze in my throat. The only thing I could hear was my erratic beating heart before the clap of his hand merged on my ass, breaking the silence. *Fuck, he wasn't kidding.* The sting across my bum by the fifth spank illuminated a frantic pulse deep inside, reducing me to a flailing mass. This was a spanking of global proportions. He didn't stop to massage the massive ache between my legs. My reeling pussy tremors rocked me to the core and I cried out in sweet agony.

He paused for a moment to rub my burning ass flesh. "Good girl. You're almost there. And then I'll let you come."

Derek's hand reinvested its maximum return on my back end. He applied quick, blunt slaps that harvested a budding pressure inside my walls. Eighteen, nineteen, and twenty were the money shots. When his fingers granted me treasured relief, I became bankrupt of my senses.

"Oh Jesus…Derek…ah… Fuck!"

Those were the only words I could utter before I broke out in shrieks of ruination. I bathed Derek in a splashing stream of juices.

He withdrew his sopping fingers and perched them on my puckering anus. "This is mine, baby. I'm in charge of training it for my cock."

His long, sizable fingers lodged inside my snug ass and I screamed his name so loud, I almost passed out. His other hand flew to my plump clit, tapping me out, draining me from end to end while he carved into my tight cavity. With a final unyielding combo of vaulting power, he obliterated me and my body cashed-out. I was spent.

He freed my wrists. "Excellent, my angel. Let's get some lotion on your bottom. Can you get up?

"Only if I can lay back down."

"Of course. I'll be right back."

I flopped down on the bed with lifeless limbs and a swirling euphoric feeling. Derek returned from the bathroom with a warm washcloth.

He soothed my freshly plunged ass. "Does that feel good?"

I purred. "Everything you do feels good."

"You're almost ready. I could feel it."

"Almost ready for what?"

He lay down next to me with the lavender lotion in his hand. "You're almost ready for me to claim you fully."

I glanced down at the comforter. "I've been thinking about it, a lot, and I–I know when I want to do it."

He tucked a finger under my chin and his eyes met mine. "When, my sweet girl?"

"On our wedding night, on Christmas Eve."

His lips caressed mine and I shivered under the tenderness of him. "That's perfect, just like you. Now let me take care of my baby."

He covered me with a generous helping of lotion and I relaxed. "Derek, can I ask you something?"

"Anything, sweetie."

"How did you get so good at everything?"

"What do you mean?"

"I mean, sex. How did you get so good at it? Did you *Google* it, or take a pussy class? You know, like, 'How to make a girl come in three easy steps.'"

He chuckled. "You still don't get it. It has nothing to do with me. It's all you."

I sat up. "Me?"

He gathered me in his arms. "Yes. The moment you let go the first night we were together, you gave yourself to me. You surrendered control. You were mine from the beginning. You've allowed us to soar to new heights. It's you."

"But still. How did you figure out…stuff?"

"Well, that's you too. You're body is so responsive and expressive. I just tune into you and you take us." He smiled and ran the back of his hand across my cheek. "I've always said, you have no idea how incredibly sexy you are. You're the one guiding me. Then I feel free to explore new pleasures, but only because you've entrusted me with your body. The most gorgeous body I've ever seen."

My skin warmed at the sound of his words. I offered him my mouth and he took it, his kiss sang through my veins. His hand roamed down my neck and skimmed my breasts. My breath released in a long surrendering moan.

He eased me on my back and continued to worship my body in featherlight kisses and arousal inducing touches. Cradled in one of his arms, he fondled one small globe until its pink nipple marbled hard. I tingled while his tongue tantalized the other bud making it peak to its fullness.

"Oh, Derek, yes. Can we keep playing? Can we play with the nipple clamps?"

He dashed off the bed to our drawer of toys, plucked up the nipple clamps and set them down next to me.

Straddling me, he said. "I want to warm you up a little bit more before we try these. If it's too much, we can stop."

I nodded and he gave me that look, love mixed with heat. Gently his hands outlined the circle of my breasts, bringing my pink tips to greater glory. He brought his mouth down on my pert little wonders and sucked them into his mouth with precise possession. It nurtured a simmering desire in my belly and flowed south. While he suckled one nipple, his fingers pinched the other roughly and I gasped. He gave each one equal treatment, preparing me for my wicked torment.

He picked up the clamps, placed them on my pointed, hard nubs without letting go. "Are you okay?"

"Yeah, they don't hurt. Is that because you're still holding on?"

"I'm actually not sure. I've never done this before. Just breathe and then I'll let go. Ready? Good girl."

Derek took his hands off the nipple clamps.

I screamed. "Motherfucker! Take them off! Fuck! Wine! Fuck!"

He removed them immediately. "Oh, God, I'm

sorry."

I rolled to my side clutching my poor, violated nips. "Who invented those? Satan?"

"Does it really hurt that bad?"

"Would you like to try them?"

"Hell, no. I believe you. Let me take a look."

I uncrossed my arms and showed him my itty-bitty-titty tips. He brushed the pad of his thumb across them. "Oh, my poor baby. They're a little bit red. I'm going to get some ice."

I handed him the clamps. "Here take these with you and throw them away. And remind me to punch Shannon in the face the next time I see her. She gave them to me."

He kissed the top of my head. "Whatever you say, my angel. Just relax. I'll be right back."

Derek returned with a bowl of ice and a towel. I was still flat on my back with my arms wrapped around my chest. He knelt down beside me with an ice cube in hand. "Just close your eyes and feel."

I shut my eyes and felt the biting chill of the ice touch my nipple. Derek held it there until the heat of my breast started to evaporate the cube, and it dripped and trickled on my skin. He took the frozen treat away and brought his warm mouth down on my swelling orb. My body was like ice and flame all at once. Another glacial delight cooled and cooed my other nipple. My flesh began to bubble in feverish desire. Drizzles of the melting cube broke me out in goose bumps and fired a naughty craving flittering throughout. When his mouth descended this time, I convulsed, grabbed his dark-blond hair, and held him there.

He flicked his tongue over my protruding bud, while I writhed underneath him. His mouth eased off my breast. I heard him pick up another cube and felt him astride me. "I want you to come for me."

I heaved. "Yes."

"Open your eyes. Good girl. Keep them on me."

I peered into Derek's crystal blue eyes. They sparkled in wonder as they roved over my body. He trailed the cube from sternum to my belly button, leaving a sultry, flowing sensation in its wake. Derek's tongue tickled my belly button and licked up the icy sheen of wetness.

His lips came down on mine with a passionate yearning. My hands found his toned perfect ass and I attempted to force him inside me. His cool, soft mouth was making me crazy with need.

"Derek, please," I whispered.

He sat up and pressed my wrists into the mattress. "Not until you come for me." He let go of my wrists, moved with his back against the headboard, and extended his hand.

I took his hand and straddled him. His animalistic gaze locked on my breasts and my rosy peaks grew to a pebbled hardness. "They're so beautiful. Bring them to my mouth."

I brought my breasts to him and he ravished them,

with forceful sucks and nibbles. He pinched and squeezed, while I shrieked in gleeful anguish. His thumb and forefinger rolled one erect teat. This time when he took it in his mouth, he suctioned my nipple firmly between his lips, making me mewl. His tongue lashed over my breasts and he barred his teeth, holding me to him. Gentle bites compelled my body to amp up in a different way. My hands dove into Derek's hair as the tension from my impending climax wrenched me to my core. With just a few more titillating tastes, I let go, shattering in a million glowing stars.

My cheek rested on his chest. "Oh my God. I never felt anything like that before. It was incredible."

"You're the incredible one, my sweet girl." He positioned me so his tip rested at my entrance. "I can't wait any longer."

"I can't either. All night it's been about making me come. You have amazing self-control."

He gripped my hips. "Did you say control? Who's in control right now, Nia?"

I blew out a ragged breath. "You are."

"Good girl."

He spread my wet folds and pushed inside with his veins bulging along my slick walls. His rock-hard length filled me. He guided me up down while my drenched slit wetted his cock. Derek was in control. He was the commander of my heart, the keeper of my soul, the love of my life.

Chapter Eight

"You really can't skip the meeting?" Brooke was in my office, changing the plan. It was two days after her party. Derek was back in LA. Jake was with Lacey, and I needed to shop for a wedding dress. Julia and Phillip were in California, and Brooke said she would come with me. According to Derek, it wasn't safe for me to go anywhere alone.

"I'm sorry. I know I'm moving your cheese and you hate that, but my head chef wants to meet to discuss the holiday menus. Trust me, I'd rather go to Downtown Summerlin with you. What kind of dress are you looking for?"

"I might not want an actual wedding dress, just something classy and sexy, that will turn Derek to mush."

"You turn Derek to mush every time he looks at you."

"You really think so?"

"Oh come on. You'd have to be blind not to notice."

Walter James appeared in the open doorway. "Nia, can I talk to you… Oh, hey, Brooke. Do you mind if I talk to Nia in private."

I looked to Brooke as if to say stay put. "Walter, I

would feel more comfortable if Brooke stayed."

He sighed and approached my desk. "Okay, I get that. I just wanted to say I'm sorry about what happened at Brooke's party.

"What happened at my party?" Brooke asked.

"Nothing," I responded.

"Anyway," Walter continued. "I wanted to let you know I'm going back to California for awhile."

"California?" I replied. "Is that where you're from?"

"Yeah. I need to sort out a few things."

What did Derek do? "Are you going because you want to, or because Derek said something to you?"

"Derek did mention it would be best if I steered clear from you, but that's not the only reason. Things in Vegas have gotten a little complicated. The original reason I came isn't…well… I just came to tell you I'm sorry and say goodbye."

Brooke rose from her seat and embraced him. "Hey, Walter, take care of yourself. Everyone at the club will miss you."

"Thanks, Brooke. I appreciate that."

I stayed put. "Take care, Walter."

He turned to go and stopped. "For what it's worth, Nia, I think you're a good person. You and Derek deserve to be happy together. I hope that happens for you." He slunk out of the office.

Once he was out of earshot, Brooke said, "That was weird. Even for him."

"I know. I guess Lacey was right. Walter the Weird."

"What was he talking about? Did something happen at the party?"

I never told Brooke about the shredded Stargazer lilies, or Walter, or the Red Riding Hood I imagined. Her party was such a hit. Why taint it with my drama? "No. He seemed to be overreacting today like a giant lady with PMS."

"Seems like it. Sorry about the shopping. Do you want to go later in the week? Oh no. I know that look."

"What look?"

"It's the look you get when you're determined to not change the plan. Nia, you can't go alone, you do realize that?"

"Well, think about it—"

"Oh, here we go again."

"Since Jake thought I was going to be with you, and I gave him the night off, I can get someone from security to drive me home."

"Nia, I can drive you home. That's why I came over here. My car is right outside. I just can't go shopping."

"No, it's fine. I can radio the booth. Then I'll only go to Nordstrom's. I'll park my car close to the door, have a quick look around, and come right home."

"I don't think that's a good idea."

I grabbed up my stuff. "Will you shut the door for me and turn out the light?"

"Nia. Stop. Are you sure you know what you're doing?"

"It's just Nordstrom's. Nordstrom's is good for the soul. It'll be fine."

"Just promise me you'll be careful."

"I promise. I'll touch base with you as soon as I leave the store."

I flew around the corner and nearly smacked into Shannon. "Shannon, I'm sorry. I didn't see you there."

"Where are you off to in such a hurry?"

"Um…I'm…just anxious to get home to Molly. She misses Derek."

"I was actually looking for you. Walter is taking me out tonight, just the two of us. He said he has something special to discuss. I'm so excited. I hope he wants us to move in together."

I didn't have the heart to tell her, Walter was about to break her heart. I fled. "Oh wow! Have fun!"

* * * *

The second I walked into the door Molly bounded toward me. She moved as if she still weighed fifteen pounds. Sometimes her gangling limbs threw her off-balance. It was a funny stage. She wasn't quite used to her adolescent maturity.

After a quick cuddle, my phone rang. "Hey, Aunt Mary Jane. How are you?"

"Well, is the wedding on or off?"

"Ha, ha, very funny. It's still on." When Derek and I broke up, I talked to Aunt Mary Jane nearly every day. She would tell me we had a once in lifetime kind of love and would get back together. When we did get back together, she said she was going to choreograph a special "told you so" dance.

"Oh good."

"Did you get the date for Uncle Bill's knee surgery? I'm really glad you talked him into it."

"Yes, and that's why I'm calling. It's December 18. He'll be out of the hospital, but won't be in any condition to fly. I'm sorry. It looks like we won't be able to come to the wedding. I kind of held off on pushing for it, but you and Derek broke up and his knee got worse…"

"It's okay. I understand. Our friends Steve and Scott can't come either. They didn't even make it to Brooke's engagement party. Life is all about taking care of each other. And you need to take care of your snoring clodhopper."

"Oh you're right, but I hate that I'm missing it. Plus, the snoring clodhopper is the world's worst patient. He had a cataract removed last year and bumbled around the house like Helen Keller. I had to do everything for him. I'll never forget it. He knocked over a full jug of water and was standing next to the paper towels. I told him to hand me the roll and he gives me one lousy paper towel. What the fuck am I supposed to do with that? I hate to break it to you, Nia, but that's men for you. They like to bring a knife to a gun fight."

I cracked up. "I'll have to remember that. Maybe early next year we can get away for a weekend and come visit. When Uncle Bill feels up for it."

"We would love it."

No sooner had I hung up when the bell rang. It was Marshall with my Stargazer lilies. "Hey, come on in."

"Sorry, I didn't get these to you yesterday. The cleanup from Brooke and Tom's party was brutal. Where did you two run off to?"

"Oh… We both got hot in our costumes and came on home. I guess we missed all the fun."

Marshall and I headed back to the kitchen. "You certainly did. By the end of the evening, Brooke and I practically traded costumes, I make a hideous blond, and Tom's Uncle Shelley grabbed Julia's ass. It was hilarious."

"Sounds like it. Oh, and if you're looking for Derek, he's not here. He went back to LA."

He blushed. "Does that mean Jake's here?"

"No. Sorry, he's with Lacey. Actually, that reminds me. Brooke was going to come help me look for a wedding dress at Downtown Summerlin, but she has a meeting. Do you want to come with me?"

"Nothing would make me happier, but I still have a few more deliveries. I heard that Nordstrom's was to die for. You should go for it and have fun."

"I think I will. Downtown Summerlin, here I

come."

* * * *

I pulled my Honda into a space right by the door. A pang of guilt consumed me. I really shouldn't be doing this. Derek would flip if he knew, so I decided to send a text to Jake, just to cover my ass. I sent it, turned off my phone, and hurried inside.

Marshall was right. This Nordstrom's was to die for. It was like the mother ship was calling me home. My senses were on overload taking in the grand beauty. It still had that new store smell.

The sign said "Special Occasion Dresses" with an arrow pointing to the right, so I headed in that direction. Luckily, there were rows and rows of holiday dresses. I just needed to find the perfect one to wear when I married Derek on Christmas Eve. The task proved more difficult than I originally thought.

I turned to find someone to help me and gasped. Sonya was in the store with her head craning about, as if she was looking for someone. Was that someone me? I ducked behind a rack of sequined cocktail dresses and ran the length of the wall to the door. I made it through the junior department with my heart hammering in my chest. What the fuck is she doing here? It's as if she knew I'd be in this store. I was almost at the door when she landed in front of me.

I exhaled. "Sonya, I have a restraining order out

against you. You need to leave me alone."

She clasped her hands together. "Please, Nia, I'm trying to help you. I'm risking going to jail, just to talk to you."

"No! Please, leave me alone." I bolted past her.

She shouted after me, "You have friends that aren't really your friends. They are trying to hurt you."

I ran to my car and peeled out in a blind panic. What did she mean? Who is trying to hurt me? How did she know I'd... Brooke...? Brooke was the only person I told I was going to Nordstrom's. She wouldn't, would she? My mind darted back and forth about Sonya's phone calls and having coffee with her. And then there was the Little Red Riding Hood I saw at her party. Brooke also knew about the Stargazer lilies. *Oh my God.* Brooke was the one that never threw my original application away, and Sonya found it and gave the information to Larry Wall. Was Sonya talking about her? As I drove, I grew more furious. The pieces fitted together so clearly. It had to be Brooke.

I pulled my car right next to Brooke's in the country club parking lot. For her sake, her meeting better be over. I passed the head chef on the way into her office.

"Brooke, I need to talk to you."

"I'm so glad to see you. Sonya just called me. She feels terrible for scaring you at Nordstrom's."

"She feels terrible? What about you? Do you feel anything?"

"I don't know what you're talking about."

"I'm talking about your best friend Sonya. When I spotted her, it looked like she knew I'd be there. Like maybe someone tipped her off."

Brooke didn't flinch. "Nia, do you want something to drink? Maybe you should sit down."

"No, I don't want anything, except the truth."

"What truth? You're not making any sense."

"I want to know why every time something happens to me, you're involved. My application that Sonya found led Nick to me. The security breeches that no one can seem to figure out. The phone calls from Sonya, which you could ignore by the way, and don't."

"Are you accusing me of something?"

"Should I be? Don't you think this seems awfully suspicious? I didn't want to tell you this, but the night of your party someone left shredded Stargazer lilies in the private dining room. It would've had to have been someone who knew about the flowers and encouraged Derek and I to go in there. I was by myself and could've sworn I saw Little Red Riding Hood leaving the room. I mean, how do you explain all of this?"

Brooke grabbed her bag in a huff. "Okay, now you're just flat out talking crazy, and I don't appreciate it."

"Am I? You don't think any of this is just a little too coincidental?"

"I think you need to leave before we both say things we'll regret."

* * * *

Jake and Lacey anxiously awaited my return in the kitchen. When I walked in the door, I felt like a teenager out past her curfew.

Anger gripped Jake's face. "What the fuck, Nia. Are you trying to get me fired? You're phone is turned off. You might want to turn it back on. You have a few messages from me, and from Derek."

"Derek? You called him? You told on me?"

"What was he supposed to do?" Lacey asked. "You sent that text and turned off your phone. We've been crazy worried. We left the restaurant in the middle of dinner and went to Nordstrom's to look for you, and you weren't there, which freaked us out even more."

"Oh, I'm sorry. Brooke canceled on me at the last minute. I thought it would be fine. That it wouldn't be a big deal. I guess I fucked-up. What did Derek say?"

Jake shook his head. "He was pissed at both of us, again. He's flying back to Vegas, right now."

"Oh shit! You got to believe me, I didn't mean for any of this to happen. I'll explain to Derek that this was my fault."

Everything that transpired in the last hour closed in on me—Sonya, the fight with Brooke, and now Derek coming home with a full head of steam. I sank down in one of the kitchen chairs and stared at the table.

Lacey sat down next to me. "Hey, are you all right?

You look like you're going to cry. Did something happen?"

"I don't want to talk about it."

She started to get up and I grabbed her hand. "Can you guys just sit with me for awhile?"

"Sure, of course we can. Anything you need? Do you want some wine?" Lacey asked.

"Yes, please. Wine sounds perfect."

* * * *

After two glasses of wine, and the stress of the day, I was wiped out. Lacey and Jake stayed downstairs waiting for Derek to come home. I retreated to my bedroom with Molly. Maybe if I was asleep he wouldn't be so hard on me.

Fuck! Of course I couldn't sleep. My head twirled with thoughts of Sonya, my fight with Brooke, and my impending doom.

The door swung open and Derek's footsteps trampled across the carpet. "Nia, are you awake?"

Molly popped up first with tail wagging enthusiasm. "How's my sweet pooch?"

I rolled over and braced myself. "If I wag my tail, will you be nice to me too?"

His tired, stern eyes met with mine. "What do you have to say for yourself?"

"That I'm really sorry I worried everyone. I'm sorry you felt like you had to stop what you're doing and fly here to yell at me."

Derek plopped down on the bed and sighed. "When Jake said you texted him that you were out alone and he couldn't reach you, I took off for the airport. So many scenarios plagued my mind. I'm at a loss."

He put his head in his hands in defeat. I frightened him to the point where he couldn't even scold me.

I sidled up next to him. "Honey, I'm sorry. But I get frustrated never being able to go out by myself. I had my mind set on going shopping, and when Brooke canceled I—"

"Didn't want to change the plan?"

"Yes. I suppose so, but it's more than that. Larry Wall went to jail, but I feel like the prisoner. It's just not fair."

"You make an excellent point, but that does not excuse your behavior. It was selfish of you to text Jake and then turn off your phone. I mean, really, the fucking phone again. I need to know I can trust you. Trust you to make good choices. When are you going to be more responsible?"

"Starting right now. You can trust me, I swear. I learned my lesson. It isn't safe for me to be alone. Something is going on. There's somebody I trust that really isn't my friend. I think it might be Brooke."

"Brooke? What are you talking about?"

"Brooke was the only person that knew I was going to Nordstrom's. I wasn't there more than five minutes before I spotted Sonya looking for me."

"Jesus, Nia. See, this is what I'm talking about."

"I know. But there's a part of me that thinks Sonya wants to help me. I mean, I'm not taking any chances and talking to her, but she said I have friends that aren't my friends. There's someone we can't trust. The more I think about it, it has to be Brooke."

"How can you say that? Think about everything she's done for you. She's every bit as loyal as Julia is. It can't possibly be her. Don't even go there. Don't say anything to her about this. Once you accuse somebody, there's no turning back."

"It's too late. I already did. We had a terrible fight. Oh God, you're right. It couldn't be Brooke. What have I done?"

"You need to fix it. First thing in the morning go to her and apologize."

"I will. Hopefully she'll understand, I freaked-out when I saw Sonya."

"Sonya may be right about one thing. There could be someone you shouldn't trust. If you ask me it's Walter. There's something about him, even Marshall said so."

"I saw Walter today. He's moving back to California. He mentioned you talked to him."

"I'm glad. There's no fucking way I was going to allow him another opportunity to touch you. It needed to be done."

"What did you do?"

"I offered him a sizable amount of cash to clear out

of our lives for good."

"How much?"

He hesitated and exhaled. "Ten thousand dollars."

"Derek, are you scared?"

He cupped my face in his beautiful hands. His eyes filled with tears. "Yes, my angel. I'm terrified someone is going to hurt you and take you away from me. Please, don't run off on your own again. Promise me you will keep your phone with you, and on at all times. I'm doing everything I can to protect you. You have to protect yourself too. I can't take this. The thought of losing you is tearing me up inside. Please, baby. Promise me."

I crawled onto his lap and he gently rocked me. "I promise. I really do. I'm scared too."

* * * *

"Brooke, what's going on?" The next morning I rushed to her office to apologize. It was empty except for the desk and chairs. Cardboard boxes stuffed to the gills were by the door.

She barely looked up from her desk. "What do you want, Nia? I'm busy."

"I came to apologize. What's with all the boxes?"

"I'm leaving."

"What do you mean, you're leaving?"

"I mean, I quit my job, and I'm leaving?"

"What? You can't quit. You love your job. Is this

because of me?"

She crossed to the boxes and placed her big key ring on top. "You know what, not everything is about you. This is about me and Tom. I'm engaged to a wonderful man that I can't be with, because of a job that I don't even need. So, I quit and I'm going to go on tour with him. I was going to do this in September, but you needed me when you and Derek broke up, so I stayed. I stayed and held your hand through all of it. I was there for you."

"I know. Thank you. I couldn't have gotten through it without you."

"And yet, you repay me by accusing me of something so vile. All I've ever done is look out for you and help you. How could you?"

"I'm so sorry. I came to apologize. You've had my back from day one. I know that. Can you forgive me?"

She hoisted a box into her arms. "I don't think so."

"Brooke, please. Don't go."

"I don't think there's anything left to say."

She turned to go and it felt like she was taking a piece of my heart with her. I couldn't let it end like this. "Brooke, wait. There's got to be something I can do to make this right."

"The damage is already done. But you could do something for me."

"Anything, just name it."

"Think before you speak. Words are like bullets. Don't just fire them off whenever you feel like it. Oh, and just so you know, the country club never wanted me to hire you because you changed your name from Meagan Ryan to Nia Kelly. They found it suspicious and I vouched for you. I also had to fight to get you the promotion to fitness coordinator. The powers that be thought you were too young for the responsibility, but I was the one that assured them you could do it. I was your friend, a really good friend. You were like a sister to me. I considered you family."

"I still am, Brooke. Please let me make it up to you."

"You can't. Just think before you speak. That's all I have to say to you. Goodbye."

Chapter Nine

"To Nia and Derek," Julia toasted. "Now, don't be a baby, Nia Kelly. Slam that Tequila shot."

It was my bachelorette party. Me and my girls were turning it up at the Barking Toad, the Friday before Thanksgiving.

Derek was in LA. He texted an hour ago that he wrapped on *First Bite*. Vampire Drake Braden was a part of his past. To celebrate, he was having dinner with Eden and her partner, Heather, at their house in Hollywood Hills. I was glad they remained friends after they ended their fake relationship for the cameras. I had yet to meet Heather, but from what Derek said, she was lovely. Eden stayed safely tucked into the closet with her secret intact.

Since Brooke and Walter left town, I hadn't experienced one suspicious or frightful moment. Maybe Larry Wall decided seeking revenge was too great a risk. Maybe I was finally safe. Of course, that didn't stop Jake from sticking to me like glue, and making sure I had my phone with me and turned on every single day.

Derek would takeover as phone cop tomorrow when I got to LA. I was flying out in the morning to spend an early Thanksgiving with his parents before they headed to Chicago to celebrate the holiday with Derek's sister, Dina and her family.

Valerie, Derek's mom, phoned earlier to say we'd be meeting at Derek's LA house with a top-notch wedding coordinator. There wasn't much to coordinate. As long as the manger scene was on the mantle with the trees on either side, it was all good. It was really happening. In a little over a month, I would be Derek Pierce's wife—the luckiest woman in the world.

The packed crowd at the Barking Toad resembled my party crew, drunk ogling women with tight skinny jeans and high spirits. Shannon wanted to go to a strip club. Sue and Julia voted for the Chippendales. It was Lacey's idea to come here. It was part nightclub, part hole in the wall bar. The male waiters were shirtless and a bevy of heavenly rippled muscle. None of them could compare to Derek, but they were nice to look at. Each one had a different theme to his costume, a Cowboy, a Fireman, the Pool Boy. It was so entertaining, watching all the women's eyes light up as they careened around the room in perfectness.

Poor Jake was babysitting all of us. It was the only way Derek would allow me to have a bachelorette party. That, and my vow to make better choices. I wanted him to trust that I would do the right thing.

Jake popped in the bar from time to time, made sure my phone was in hand, rolled his eyes at the shenanigans and left.

Lacey, Shannon, and Sue were crushing it on the

dance floor. Julia and I were at the bar. As usual, she was observing everyone's moves and delivering hilarious play by play commentary. "Okay, over by the Christmas tree that you know was up all year long, there's that blonde in the red top. Do you see her?"

"Yes. She's so drunk, she thinks the tree is a person."

"She just ordered a drink from the Cowboy. All right, wait for it… He's going in… Watch her."

The blonde tossed her hair and laughed while grabbing her shot off his tray. She took a sip, and poured the rest on his chiseled chest and licked it off.

"Oh my God." I gasped.

"I know. Lacey said sometimes the guys lay on the bar and the girls do body shots off of them. That's a clown car of crazy, I would love to see."

"Hopefully none of us will get that lit up. Although, it's nice to be out and not a soul here knows or cares I'm marrying a celebrity. I just wish…"

"You miss Brooke, don't you?"

"I do. Have you talked to her?"

"No. I tried calling and texting, but I haven't heard back. She's not even on *Facebook* anymore."

"She probably doesn't want to talk to you because of me. I really know how to fuck things up for everyone."

"Can I be totally honest?"

"Of course. Why stop now? You always give it to me straight. Go for it."

"It wasn't cool that Brooke went to coffee with Sonya. And it's weird to me that she left town so fast. Deep down, I don't think she did anything, but I do think she was a little hard on you. None of us knows what it's like to be in your shoes and constantly on pins and needles."

"Thank you for saying that. Derek thinks Walter was up to something. Maybe he was right. Not one strange thing has happened since he left town. For the first time in a long time, it's like we were in college, without a care in the world. It feels good."

"It does. We should get in so much trouble, we'll have the best make-up sex of our lives."

"Speaking of sex, did you take the advice Brooke gave you after the miscarriage? I'm sorry, maybe I shouldn't have brought it up. See, me and my big mouth."

Julia smiled. "It's fine. The world would be a boring place without you and your big mouth. And, I did listen to her. In fact, we're trying again."

"I'm so happy for you. Geez, if you get pregnant right away, I'll have to catch-up quick."

"Who knows? It might not happen for a while. This time I'm not focusing on getting pregnant, I'm focusing on having hot sex. I went back to the Adult Superstore and bought all the toys you got for your bridal shower. Did you use them?"

"We tried everything but the vibrating egg that Lacey gave me. I would give them all an A-plus. Oh, except for the nipple clamps. Maybe you have to have boobs to appreciate them, but they hurt my nips like a motherfucker."

Julia laughed. "So, you liked the butt plug?"

"Did someone say butt plug?" Sue squeezed in between us with a gleam in her eyes. "I told you, Nia, it was marvelous. Did I lie?"

"No, you did not. Thanks for coming out tonight. I'm sorry Nancy and Sharon had to miss it."

"Well, you know them. They love to go on their cruises. I like to travel sometimes. But we already live in America's playground. Hey, Pool Boy, can we please get another round of shots for me and my friends."

The tanned, barely clothed bartender grinned. "Anything for you, hot lady."

Sue giggled. "He just doubled his tip."

"You do look hot, Sue. And you looked really hot at Brooke's party," I said.

"I didn't even see you that night."

"Well, I saw you and the girls in your S and M costumes. It made me curious."

"Yeah, I was wondering if you guys were like into it for real," Julia added.

Pool Boy placed our shots in front of us. "Tequila, right, ladies?"

Sue handed him two twenties. "Oh yes. Thanks, and keep the change." She practically hyperventilated like she did when she first met Derek. "Okay, girls, do a shot with me and I'll answer your question."

"I don't know if I should," I replied. "I've already had one and I've been drinking wine. I promised Derek I wouldn't drink too much."

"Nia, just do it," Julia scolded. "It's your party. You said yourself, you want us to be like it was when we were in college."

"Fine." I slammed the shot back with scholarly skill and it burned my throat and made me shudder.

"Okay. What do you want to know?" Sue asked.

I leaned in and said softly, "Are you and Jeff into, like BDSM stuff? Marshall said there was a club in town. Have you ever been to it?"

Sue's cheeks flushed crimson. "Only once. We're just sort of interested in exploring new things."

"Good for you," Julia cheered. "I think it's good to be open to new experiences. And because of you, I am also a proud owner of a butt plug."

The Pool Boy heard Julia say butt plug and we howled with laughter.

Jake drifted into the bar to check on us and turned heads along the way. I picked up my phone off the bar and showed him. "Look, the phone is on and it's right in front of me."

"Is it locked?"

"Yes. Oh wait. I have a text from Derek." I didn't read it aloud because it said, "Just finishing dinner with Eden and Heather. When Eden gets back from shooting a movie in Canada, she would like us to double date with them. In private, of course. Is my girl behaving? I can't wait to see you tomorrow."

"What's it say?" Julia asked.

"Oh, just making sure I behave. I'll write him back in a bit." I set my phone back on the bar.

Lacey joined us and folded into Jake. "Are you checking up on us?"

He snaked his arm around her waist. "Just doing my job for Mr. Pierce. I'll head back to the car."

"Okay." She gave him a quick peck and he headed out.

"Oh, Lacey, you are one lucky lady. Damn he's hot," Sue exclaimed.

"Yep. Hot and all mine." She observed our empty shot glasses. "Hey, did you do a shot without me? Let's do another round."

Sue motioned for her new boyfriend the Pool Boy and he hopped to it. She asked Lacey, "Where's Shannon?"

"She's talking to the Firemen," Lacey responded. "Sorry to be blunt, but I hope he takes her in the bathroom and fucks her brains out. She needs to forget about Walter. God, she's been so freaking moody."

The shots landed in front us, and I picked one up. "To Shannon forgetting all about Walter."

Sue chimed in, "And to the Pool Boy."

I tossed the tequila back and shuddered a little less. *Oh fuck.* I was drunk. I picked up my phone to text Derek back. The damn auto correct turned my bad spelling into a sentence that made no sense. I deleted it, and sat the phone back down.

Julia craned her neck to getter a better view of Shannon and the Fireman. "Well, Shannon's twirling her hair around her finger and smiling, so maybe she's well on her way to erasing Walter from her mind."

"Let's hope so," Lacey replied. "I probably shouldn't tell you this, but Shannon said she, Walter and Christa were having threesomes. At first, she thought it would bring them closer, but then he moved back to California, and she hasn't heard from him. Oh, and I shouldn't tell you this either, Nia, but Christa got offered a coordinator position at the gym you used to work at on the other side of town. She's quitting."

"Good God, Lacey," Julia said. "Have another drink and tell us more."

"I know. I'm awful. I can't keep a secret to save my life, especially if alcohol is involved. Please don't tell me anything you don't want the world to know."

Shannon approached the bar with the Fireman, and a big toothy grin. The hulking Fireman whispered in my ear, "Congratulations, bride-to-be."

I turned to Shannon and asked, "What did you do?"

She beamed. "I have a surprise for you."

The Fireman grabbed a microphone from behind the long, large bar. "I need all the Barking Toad Men on top of the bar. It's time to celebrate."

The ladies lost their minds and shrieks of excited glee filled the air as the beefy waiters climbed up on top of the bar. What did this have to do with me?

"Marry You" by Bruno Mars piped through the speakers. My girls shoved me front and center, while the brawny men performed their choreographed routine. The Firemen and the Pool Boy reached for me. I was so flipping drunk, I offered up my unsuspecting hands, and they pulled me on top of the bar. The cheers escalated. Somewhere deep inside I rediscovered my musical theatre entertainer buried within and put on a show. I whipped up the crowd, the guys, and myself without falling off the bar.

When the song ended, "Sexy and I Know It" by LMFAO kicked in and of all people, Sue, jumped behind the bar and poured shots for me and my back-up dancers. The Fireman motioned for me to pour my shot on him. I went for it. Then, the ladies chanted, "Lick it up. Lick it up." What was I doing? The flat of my tongue dove to his belly button and trailed over his abs to his pecks. The room erupted in raucous cheers. He dipped me and planted his lips on mine. My head dizzied when the Fireman pulled me upright. I probably looked like a drunk deer in the headlights. Sue handed me one more shot. I regained what was left of my composure and downed it while I gyrated with my new male friends.

As Aunt Mary Jane would say, the "dirty commotions" ceased and the room quieted to a dull roar. From the bar, I spied a horrified Jake at the doorway. He fought his way through the crowd and offered me an insistent hand. The look on his face was clear. The party was over.

He helped me off the bar with a strong, firm grip, and whispered in my ear, "Okay, darling. Time to get you home. Mr. Pierce would insist."

I put my hands on his chest to steady myself. "He so would. He's freaking bossy." I slurred to the girls. "Come on, the train is leaving the station."

Jake placed his hands on my shoulders. "Nia, do you have your phone?"

"Goddamn it. My phone can suck my dick."

"I'm going to take that as a no, and just assume your Tequila is talking for you." He called to Lacey, "Can you find Nia's phone?"

In my drunken haze, I think I heard her say, "Got it. She left it on the bar."

At least I wasn't the only shit-faced one in the bunch. We all practically fell into the car.

Lacey couldn't resist teasing Shannon. "So, did you get the Fireman's phone number?"

"No. He asked me if I wanted to see his hose, though."

Lacey laughed. "You should've had a quickie in the bathroom."

Sue added, "Or at least have him get you off. Two in the pink, one in the stink. Works every time."

We busted a gut and Julia chimed in, "Two in the goo, one in the poo!"

I doubled over in drunken hysterics. Our laughter subsided and Jake's voice boomed into the backseat.

"Ladies, I can hear you."

The hysterics continued all the way home.

* * * *

"How come you don't seem that drunk?" Lacey was putting Molly and me to bed.

"Well, for starters, you weigh no pounds, and I don't think I drank as many shots as you. Nice show you put on. What was it like, licking that guys chest?"

"I licked someone?"

"Yes. The Fireman on top of the bar. I guess you don't remember him kissing you either?"

The Tequila buzz began to subside. "Oh shit. Did that really happen?"

"Uh, yes. It's okay. My boyfriend came to your rescue before things got out of control."

"Jake is so good to me. I mean, at first, it was weird to have him in the house when Derek was away, but now I like it. I like it when you stay too."

Lacey sat on the bed. "So, no more accidental naked sightings?"

"Thank God, no. Once was plenty." I nestled into my pillow. "I think I'm starting to fade."

"Okay. You've got your water and the trash can by the bed. Need anything else?"

I popped up. "Oh no. My phone. Shit."

"Relax. I picked up your phone. It's on the nightstand. I checked it. It needs charging. Do you want me to get your charger?"

"No. That's okay."

"Don't forget, Jake and I are leaving early to head for the airport. Thanks for the time off. He's meeting my parents in Colorado."

My eyelids were so heavy. I couldn't stay awake. "No problem. Have a good meet…"

"Goodnight, Nia. Let me know if you need anything."

There was only one thing I needed, not to have a hangover in the morning.

Chapter Ten

"Nia!" Derek yelled my name louder than usual. Oh, my fucking head felt like it had been bashed by a baseball bat.

"Nia! What the fuck did you do?"

What is he doing here? I was supposed to meet him. Why does he sound so mad?

He burst through the door. "Get up. You've got some explaining to do."

I couldn't pry my head off my pillow. "Derek, I… Shit."

"Perfect. On top of everything else, you're hungover. Well, that's just fucking great."

"Why are you yelling so loud?"

He grabbed my arms and yanked me upright. "You want to know why. Take a good look. These pictures are everywhere."

Through squinted, bleary eyes, I peered at the pictures on Derek's screen. As my focus sharpened, it became clear. Oh, no. I'd really gone and done it this time. "Is that me? On top of a bar?"

"On top of a bar and licking a Fireman's chest. You want to tell me exactly what the fuck you were thinking? The headline reads, 'Derek's Pierce's Fiancée Parties Hard in Vegas. Is The Wedding Still On?'"

"I…don't know what to say. I was just blowing off steam. I swear, I didn't see anyone take pictures."

"I suppose it was hard to see while making a spectacle of yourself. Christ, Nia. My parents are going to see this. Everyone will see it. I've been on the phone with my team all morning trying to squelch it, and it's not happening."

I hung my head in disgrace. "I'm sorry. Oh God, I think I'm going to be sick." I hurled into the trash can next to the bed. I always cried when I threw up. Perhaps it was the violent extraction of the burning vomit.

Derek had zero compassion for me. "Jesus, how much did you have to drink? You didn't even text me back last night. I was worried sick until I heard from Jake."

"I can't remember."

"Did you remember to keep your phone locked and with you?"

I flattened back on the bed and lied my ass off. It was my only defense. "Yes."

"You better not be lying to me. Where's your phone?"

I whimpered, "It's on the nightstand."

"Jesus, fucking Christ, Nia," he screamed.

"Please stop yelling at me. My head hurts."

He ordered, "Sit up, right now. I have something to show you."

I sat up as best I could, trembling. Derek had never been this angry before. "Look what's on your goddamn phone. These are the pictures that went viral. They were taken with your phone. So, you've lied to me again." He scrolled through them. "At least the photo of you kissing the Fireman didn't go viral. Is this your way of making better choices?"

He threw the phone on the bed and stormed out of the room. I picked it up and checked the pictures. Who in the hell took them? How did they end up everywhere? I'd massively screwed-up so hard. This was bad, on so many levels.

Derek returned with bottled water and Molly on her leash. "I'm flying back to LA. I'm so angry. I have to get out of here."

I clutched a pillow to my chest. "Please, stay."

"Is that what you would do if you saw me in photos kissing and licking another woman? You'd be out the door so fast, you'd never give me a chance to explain. Just like when…"

"When what? Is this payback because I ran away when I saw you kissing Mandy?"

"Maybe I've just fucking had it."

"But you can't leave. Jake's out of town. I'll be all alone."

He pressed his lips together. His eyes were cold and distant. "I don't know if I can worry about that anymore."

My jaw quivered. "Are you taking Molly to LA with you?"

"Yes."

Tears spilled down my cheeks. "Please don't take her. Derek, please. I'm sorry. I'm sorry about everything. Please don't do this. You promised you wouldn't let go, no matter what."

"You made promises too. You didn't keep any of them."

"I fucked-up, but I didn't do anything malicious on purpose. Taking Molly away from me is…" I crawled off the bed, onto the floor and hugged her tight. I broke down in sobs. "Please, let her stay here with me. I'm begging you."

"It's out of the question. You're a mess. You can't take care of her. You can't even take care of yourself. Come on, Molly."

They headed out.

"Derek! Don't go."

Without turning around, he said sternly, "I have to. I can't be around you right now."

* * * *

I curled up into the fetal position, bawling my eyes out for an hour after Derek left. Then, I hauled myself back in bed and slept the day away.

By evening, I managed a shower and made some toast. I couldn't keep it down, so I went back to bed.

When Sunday afternoon rolled around my hangover from hell morphed into the flu from hell. Derek was right. I couldn't take care of myself. I couldn't even call anyone to take care of me. They all fled out of town early for Thanksgiving. Shannon was the only person still in Vegas, and she had to hold down the fort at the club for everyone.

I kept my phone glued to me, but didn't hear a peep from Derek. I couldn't believe we were back in such an awful place. My emotions bounced between regret, fury, and sorrow. I missed Molly. How could he take her away from me?

I racked my brain, trying to figure out who took the pictures and sent them everywhere. I just hoped they didn't see the text from Derek about Eden and her partner, Heather. The culprit could have been anyone when I was up on the bar, but Lacey had my phone. She wouldn't, would she? I put it out of my mind. I already lost one friend by being suspicious, I wasn't about to lose anyone else.

I thought I would feel better by Monday morning, but I was worse. My fever spiked. Every time I ate something, I threw it right back up. I was supposed to relieve Shannon at the club in the afternoon. I picked up my phone. It was almost dead. I started to text her when it slipped out of my hand. I was so dizzy. *Oh fuck.* I couldn't...reach...

* * * *

"Baby? Oh shit. I should've never left you. Nia, can you hear me, sweetie? I'm here. I brought Molly home where she belongs."

Derek's words barely registered in my nearly comatose state. It physically hurt to open my eyes, but I wrestled them open and squeaked out, "You didn't need to come." A rattling cough shook my body and I sneezed. "I can take care of myself."

He handed me the tissues. "How's that working out for you?"

"I'm fine. I just have a little cold." Another phlegm producing cough racked me. I was burning up and freezing at the same time, but I was so mad at him, I couldn't let this get the best of me.

"You're not fine. You're stubborn as hell, but, my angel, you're sick. Let me take care of you."

I hauled myself upright. "No. You left. I begged you not to go. You don't get to come in here and…" My cough overtook me. I grew more light-headed, and fell back on the bed, hacking up a third lung.

Molly jumped up and reclined across me. It was as if she tried to quiet the cough. I missed her so much. I lost it. "Good girl, Molly." Exuberant kisses lapped up my tears.

"Come on, Molly." He picked her up and put her on the floor.

"Why did you do that?" I sobbed. "You're mean. You know that? You're so mean to me. I try to do the right thing. I have to walk on eggshells around you, and all you are is mean. How could you take Molly away from me?" I whipped myself into hysterics. "You're the meanest man in the whole world, Derek Pierce. You're so fucking mean."

He grabbed my wrists. "Nia, stop. You have to calm down. I wanted Molly to get off the bed, so you would drink the water on your nightstand. You barely touched it."

"You're not the boss of me. I don't have to listen to you."

He handed me the water. "You're going to listen to me, or I'm going to take you to the hospital. I suggest you drink up."

I downed the water quickly, even though it irritated the crap out of my sore throat. He touched his cheek to my forehead. "God, you're burning up. How long have you been running a fever?"

"Since yesterday afternoon."

"Why didn't you call me?"

"Why did you leave in the first place?"

"Okay. Fair enough. Have you eaten?"

I mumbled, "I don't care to discuss it."

"Hmm... I thought as much. Let's get you in the tub and I'll make you something."

As sick as I was, I still had it in me to be a smart-ass. "You can't cook."

"Fine. I'll have something delivered."

"Like what? I can't eat Grimaldi's pizza. I haven't been able to eat anything."

"Okay. I'll have groceries delivered. You should eat some soup or something."

I flopped my head back on my pillow. "I don't want grocery store soup. There's too much sodium."

"I didn't think it was possible, but you're actually feistier when you're sick." He hoisted me in his arms. "Let's go."

"Where are you taking me?"

"I told you I'm putting you in the tub. You'll feel better, I promise. You poor thing, you're little T-shirt is wet with sweat from your fever."

He placed a towel down between the two sinks and sat me on top of it. Then he turned on the bath and grabbed up two more towels. "Lift your arms for me." He stripped off my T-shirt and wrapped me in the soft fluffy towels to keep me warm. "There you go. That's a good girl."

A small part of me wanted his arms around me instead of the towels, but I was still pissed. "Why did you come back?"

"Shannon called me. She said you didn't show up to the club and you didn't respond to text messages or phone calls. I was worried."

"I thought you said you couldn't worry anymore."

"I said that in anger. I didn't mean it. I should've stayed." He cupped my face. "Please forgive me. I was wrong and I'm sorry."

The warmth in those ice-blue eyes melted me. "I'm sorry too. I made bad choices."

"We both made bad choices."

"So, you're not mad at me anymore?"

"No, baby. I realize now that I overreacted. My mom set me straight."

"Your mom? I thought your parents would disown me."

"Not a chance. They were both upset at me for leaving with Molly. They really wanted to see you. It's been too long."

"What did your mom say?"

"She reminded me that you're twenty-five and you're entitled to have a crazy bachelorette party. And that the only reason it was a problem was because of my career, which I chose and you didn't."

I managed to crack a smile. "Your mom is the smartest woman alive."

He drew me into his big strong arms. "You may be right about that. Keith let me have it too. You might be the most loved woman alive. I know I do. I love you, but…"

I broke our embrace. "But, what?"

He grinned. "We need to wash your hair."

"Is there throw up in it?"

"Little bit."

I covered my face with my hands. "Oh God, I really am a mess."

He removed them and gazed into my eyes. "But you're my mess. You're mine, Nia."

This man just offered to wash my brown puked upon tresses. All was forgiven. "Yes, Derek. I'm yours."

My bath was ready. He turned off the water and plucked me off the sink.

I dipped a toe into the hot water and stopped. "Um, can you give me a minute? I have to go to the bathroom."

"Sweetie, I'm not leaving you. I've told you a hundred times. You can pee in front of me. It's not a big deal. Come on."

He picked me up and carried me to the toilet.

I peeked up at him. "You know I don't think I have to go anymore."

His hand caressed my face. "Do you want me to turn around?"

"Yes please."

He turned around and because he did know me better than I know myself, he also flipped on the sink.

"Thank you. And, Derek…I love you too."

* * * *

After my bath, Derek found me some warm pajamas. They were a Christmas present from Julia last year, red with green snowflakes. He dried my hair with care and put me back in bed. I did feel a little better and even ate some saltines and lime *Jell-O* with Nurse Molly tucked into my side. She enjoyed the saltines too.

"Are you eating the crackers, or is Molly?" Derek asked.

"We're sharing. She likes them."

He grinned. "You've got a little color in your cheeks. How are you feeling?"

"Better. I think my fever went down."

"Let's see." He pressed his lips to my forehead. "I think you're right. You look adorable in your Christmas pajamas."

I teased, "Oh, you're just saying that because I don't have throw up in my hair."

He cuddled in with Molly and me. "I'm just saying that because it's true."

"I thought you'd like me better out of my pajamas." I unbuttoned my top, but a cough doubled me over, along with a string of sneezes.

Derek handed me the tissues and buttoned me back up. "No naked Nia until you're better."

I blew my nose and sounded like Rudolph the Red Nosed Reindeer. "You mean you don't want to hit this?"

He chuckled. "Of course. When you're feeling better I will hit it, and fuck it, and spank it."

"That's all the incentive I need."

"Good. Can I talk you into eating some soup for me?" I made a sour face. "It's not grocery store soup. I had some chicken noodle soup sent over from the restaurant at the club."

I perked up. "Oh, I like that. Okay. Yes please."

He popped off the bed. "You got it. Stay put and I'll bring it to you. Then I want you to take some cough syrup and go right to sleep."

"You won't get any arguments from me, ever again."

He arched his brow. "Did I just hear you right?"

"Derek, I'm serious. I don't want to fight anymore. When you walked out it crushed me and took me back to that dark place when we broke up. I can't go through that again."

He knelt on the bed and took my hands in his. "You won't. You have my word. Life throws us curve balls and I have to realize they aren't the end of the world. We can get through anything as long as we do it together. I'm going to marry you on Christmas Eve, Nia Kelly. Do you still want that?"

"I do."

Chapter Eleven

"Happy Thanksgiving, my angel." Derek nibbled my shoulder and clutched me close.

It was our first Thanksgiving together. I was in prime health and ready to celebrate with my almost husband. The countdown to our wedding was on. I just needed to get a dress. Derek's mom took care of everything else.

Our guest list shrank to six people, Derek's parents, Julia, Phillip, Keith, and Tim. As long as the minister, the manger scene, and Derek were there, I was good.

I rolled over and touched my fingertips to his chest. "Happy Thanksgiving. It's our first one."

He kissed the top of my head. "And it's just the two of us."

Molly pushed in between us, giving us kisses. "Make that the three of us," I added.

"Yep, Thanksgiving with my two favorite girls."

Derek's phone rang and interrupted our group snuggle. He checked it. "It's Eden. She probably wants to say Happy Thanksgiving. I'll be two minutes."

"Hey, yes. I was just lying in bed with Nia and Molly. No, it's fine. I'm always glad to hear from you."

While Derek chatted with Eden, I got a naughty notion. I hopped out of bed, grabbed a dog toy, and threw it down the hall for Molly. Then sauntered back to the bed and stripped out of my pajamas, putting on a little show for Derek.

His eyes grew wild with delight when I was completely naked caressing my breasts. I slithered to the bed and ripped back the covers. As suspected, his alarm cock was at attention. I climbed on top of him and he gave me a stern warning with a nod of his head. I was interested in his other head, so I sucked it into my defiant mouth.

He hissed. "Oh...yes... No, I told her and we will get...ah...together..."

I giggled on his cock. He pulled himself out of my mouth and off the bed. I sank to my knees, guzzling him back inside. Slapping my hands on his magnificent, sculpted cheeks, I secured him in place.

"Yes...I'm still here. Sorry, Molly jumped up on the bed and landed on my...ah...funny bone."

Even though Derek's "funny bone" was gorged deep in my throat, I couldn't help but chuckle. It had been awhile since I treated him to a fine face fucking. Once his free hand gripped the back of my head, I knew it wouldn't be long. I sucked in a breath, opened the back of my throat and his tip tickled my tonsils. My mouth filled with saliva, blanketing his cock in a liberal portion of slippery goodness. It was time for the mack daddy fusion of my hand and mouth, working him in long firm strokes. Boy, Eden was chatty. I could hear her voice chirping away, while Derek reduced his responses to grunts of agreement.

I brought one hand around to cup his balls, slid my middle finger along his perineum and Derek imploded instantly. "Fuck...ah... The phone's on mute. Jesus, fuck."

I sucked down his gooey, spunk delicacy with giddy pride. Then came off him and tongued the residual drippings like a kitten lapping up milk.

I peeked up at him and he shook his head with a beaming devilish grin. If payback was a bitch then my pussy was the biggest bitch in the land.

"Okay, yes, my love to Heather. I'll tell her. Bye." He threw his phone on the bed. "Well, somebody must be feeling a hundred percent with such a mischievous start to the day."

I shrugged and licked my lips. "I'm so thankful for your cock, I couldn't help myself."

He joined me on the floor with hooded excited eyes. "You know what I'm thankful for? Your pussy."

I shrieked in glee and jumped up. "No, wait. I have to call Aunt Mary Jane."

Derek caught me by my waist, tickling and teasing me. I couldn't stop laughing. "Derek. Wait. She's expecting my call."

"You should have thought about that before you deep throated me while I was talking to Eden." He plopped me down on the corner of the bed and retrieved my phone. "Go ahead, call Aunt Mary Jane. I don't mind."

"Um...I'll call her later."

"Smart girl. Now open yourself for me. Show me what's mine."

I splayed out my legs and spread my cunt lips with my fingers.

He descended to the floor with that look. "Beautiful. You're such a wicked girl, Nia Kelly. It's time to teach you and your pussy a lesson."

His tongue ran the length of my wet crease. The involuntary tremors of arousal began. I exhaled and my hands flew to my pebbling nipples.

Derek stopped. "Baby, bring your fingers back down here. I want you to spread those lips, and nice and wide."

Pure need oozed through me as I obeyed him. Using both hands, I pried my pussy flesh wide and dug my heels into the edge of the mattress. My protruding clit jutted forth like a fiendish little tower of bubbling desire.

"Hmm...excellent. Hold still for me. You're going to be punished for that little stunt you pulled while I was on the phone."

I released a long surrendering breath and Derek clamped his mouth down on my clit. It was the most exquisite torment I'd ever felt. He munched on my nub as if it was the tastiest snack he'd ever eaten. My body reveled in the vortex between pain and pleasure. I remained still, absorbing and reeling under his mastery, but my cries of passion could not be muzzled. They resounded in the room, so loud, Molly barked at the door.

His mouth eased off my clit and two fingers plunged inside my trickling hole. Once his tongue flickered on my clit like a crackling flame, that mighty build up vibrated within.

"Oh God. Derek... Ah...I've learned my lesson. I'm so close. Can I come?"

Derek kept up thrusting his fingers and rose from the floor. "Look at me, sweetie. Because you were a good girl and asked, yes, you can come. Shower me with your cum."

He knelt down and submerged his face into my pussy. An electric shock of pleasure torched me. My body convulsed, jerked, and rolled right off the bed. "Ouch! Oh fuck!"

Derek picked me up, tossed me on the bed and declared, "Five-second rule!" His face dove between my legs. He was laughing and licking while I cracked up and climaxed. It was glorious and hilarious. It was us.

My giggles subsided. "Five-second rule? I've never had a chuckle and an orgasm before."

He gathered me to him. "Well, stick with me, kid. You'll experience all kinds of new things."

I nuzzled into his neck. "I already have. I love it when we play."

His mouth came down on mine for a soft kiss. "Then we'll play all day today. I want our first

Thanksgiving to be one we'll remember for years to come. It's up to you if there will be more punishments today. Young lady, what's that look for?"

"I'm thinking."

* * * *

Later in the kitchen, I fired up the oven. Since it was just the two of us, I decided on turkey, Brussels sprouts, smashed sweet potatoes, and my one indulgence, cheesy corn in the *Crock-Pot.* Cheesy corn was like me, so bad it was good. It was simple too. I would plop frozen corn in the *Crock-Pot* with cream cheese, butter, and whatever cheese I could get my hands on. I roasted my Brussels sprouts in the oven and drizzled them in my homemade balsamic glaze, then added cranberries and slivered almonds.

My turkey prep was complete. I grabbed a large water bottle out of the fridge, opened it, took a sip, and placed it on the island.

Even though I was wearing my short cotton black robe, with the oven on I perspired. It was one of those seventy-degree November days in Las Vegas.

Derek and Molly bounded into the kitchen from their walk. "Wow. It's hot in here. We might have to turn on the air-conditioner."

Molly guzzled a big drink from her dish and trotted right outside. "You're right, it is hot in here. Molly's got the right idea. Do you want to open up the patio doors?"

"Sounds like a plan." He flung open the doors. "Did you call Aunt Mary Jane and Uncle Bill?"

"Yes. But they must've already headed to their neighbors. I'll try again tonight. Did you talk to your family?"

"Yep. Everyone says hi. Hey, I think I'll open up the patio doors upstairs too."

"Good idea. You'll need the key. I rifled through the kitchen drawer and found it. When I handed it to Derek, the sleeve on my robe caught the water bottle and dumped it all over the floor.

"Oh shit. Sorry. Derek can you hand me the roll of paper towels?"

He gave me one stinking paper towel. I thought about what Aunt Mary Jane said. Derek just brought a knife to a gunfight. I stood in the puddle of water and laughed my head off.

"What's so funny?"

"Oh nothing." Then a genius idea popped into my head. "You know, since it's so hot in here, I thought we could celebrate Naked Thanksgiving." I tore off my robe and allowed it to soak up the spilled water.

Derek flashed me a delicious grin. "Naked Thanksgiving. I love it. Does Hallmark make a greeting card for that?"

"They totally should. Happy Naked Thanksgiving. Be careful basting your bird. You wouldn't want to splash you giblets."

"God I love you." He swept me into his arms and deposited me on the island. His eyes filled with lust as he stripped off his T-shirt throwing it on top of my robe. The rest of his clothes hit the floor, collecting up any extra spilled water.

His hands landed on the outside of my thighs as he leaned in. "I'm going to go upstairs and open up the doors. You're going to sit here and wait for me." He lightly touched his lips to each nipple. "You may play with your breasts, but nothing else. Now, let me have a look." I opened my legs and he checked my wetness. "Good girl. I'll know if you disobeyed me."

He granted me a quick peck and then it dawned on me. "Derek. There's just one problem."

"What's that, sweetie?"

"The turkey has to go in the oven."

He smirked. "Very well."

My eyes delighted in his Viking-like frame sliding the bird inside. Before he left the kitchen, he took my mouth by surprise in a succulent kiss that made me hotter than the oven. I coiled my legs around his waist, pressing my increased dewiness against him.

He broke the kiss and gave me a heated glare. "Remember the rules. I'll be right back."

Once I heard his footsteps rounding the corner, I flattened back on the island and had a go at myself. I was so amped up, I hit my head on the bottle of olive oil, and didn't give two shits. Maybe I could rub one out fast and he would never know. My nervy fingers were sucked inside my now sopping hole. I humped rigorously on one hand, while rubbing my clit like a horny demon. Oh God, I was climbing to the point of no return. A truck could hit me and I wouldn't be able to stop. I closed my eyes while I defiled myself to the edge. *Fuck yes.* This was so bad, it was so good—like me and the *Crock-Pot* of cheesy corn. I tapped my clit just as Derek would, and an outpouring of juices spurted forth. There was plenty more where that came from. I wanted to watch my radiant stream, so I opened my eyes and lifted my head. Derek was perched between my legs.

His steely blue eyes bore down on my flagrant act of rebellion. "Please, don't let me stop you."

It may have been a test. A test I was about to fail. *Oh well, F stands for fuck.* I continued my disregard for his rules. My pussy was as insubordinate as I was. It shot a triumphant fountain of cum, drenching Derek in its wake. Talk about a watershed moment. Our eyes remained locked on one another, while my impassioned shrieks echoed in the kitchen.

I collapsed on the island with my lifeless limbs dangling in satisfaction. I heaved. "Well, since I was probably going to be punished today, I decided to go out with a bang. I don't like to do anything half-assed."

Derek closed in on me. "Half-assed. Hmm… interesting choice of words. Come on. Let's get in the shower." He lifted me off the island and carried me upstairs. "That was an impressive display of disobedient squirting."

"I know, right? If Noah from the bible had been there he would've started collecting animals two by two."

"That's my girl."

Once we got in the shower, I plied him with questions. "So, what's going to be my punishment? Please tell me you chucked those nipple clamps."

He threw his head back and laughed. "For such a bad girl, you're awfully inquisitive. I'm going to make you wait, since patience isn't your strong point."

"No, it sure isn't, neither is being flexible or keeping my mouth shut."

He plucked up my washcloth and cleansed my sex. "But this, my pussy, is extraordinary."

I flung my arms around his neck. "It kind of is. You literally tapped into something I didn't know was possible. I like to think of it as the super soaker."

"Very accurate indeed." His arms snaked around my waist and he held me close. The hot rush of the shower, the scent of Jasmine Vanilla and Derek toted us back to our bubble. I was safe, and together we were untouchable.

* * * *

I was bent over, basting the turkey when Derek came behind me and stroked my backside. "You have such a sweet little ass, baby. I can't wait to spend all day disciplining it."

His words alone sprouted a warming sensation coasting through me. I shut the oven and turned to him. "What do you think of Naked Thanksgiving so far?"

"Naked Thanksgiving is so amazing. I was wondering how you'd feel about Naked Christmas and Naked New Year?"

I clutched his bum. "Let's just make all the holidays naked! I can hardly wait for Arbor Day."

"You've got yourself a deal."

I gave him a quick peck. "Actually, we've got ourselves a mess. I better clean the kitchen, and Molly needs her lunch."

"I fed Molly while you dried your hair."

"Oh well, still, look at the kitchen floor. It's a mess."

"Not so fast." He grabbed my hand and penetrated me with his eyes. It was on and I was his for the taking. He welded our bodies together and captured my mouth in a raw act of possession. My entire being succumbed to his will. His hands wandered freely over my back and bottom, creating a heated tingle low in my belly. Little by little, he guided me out of the kitchen and into the TV room. The back of my knees bumped into the armrest of the couch. We moaned into each other's mouths while my tongue surrendered to his. My fingers dug into his tussled dark-blond hair while he pressed our yearning bodies together.

His hand flew to my chin and he heaved. "It's time

for you punishment, Nia. Turn around and bend over. I have a surprise for you."

His eyes filled with so much lust I could have evaporated into a puddle. With a thumping heart, I turned around and bent over, offering myself up to my titillating fortune. The second he palmed my ass cheeks every cell in me surged in sinful anticipation.

He split mc open with his fingers and blew a light breeze over my sex. His tongued teased my slit, juicing me up until tiny drizzles leaked out.

"Excellent, my angel. I need you to trust me. Spread yourself nice and wide for me and keep your hands there.

I reached around and pulled myself open for him. "I trust you."

"That's, my good girl."

He wedged a warm, slippery foreign object deep inside my inner cavity. It felt weird, but in a good, bad girl kind of way. I knew it was probably Lacey's gift, the vibrating egg.

"Okay, you can stand up and turn around now."

When I faced him, there was a glimmer of impishness in the corners of his mouth, but his stare remained full of intensity.

He opened up his hand revealing something familiar. "This is the remote control for the gift Lacey got you. That's what's inside you. You are not to remove it. Only I can. Understand?"

I teased, "I understand, Mr. Pierce. You'll get no

trouble from me."

He grinned and drew me to him. "You are trouble. And I love it. Now march your pretty ass into the kitchen." He swatted my behind.

With just two steps, the trouble in my loins began. The weighted feeling inside me created a perplexing sizzle. Derek hit the remote, stopping me in my tracks as the vibration fired through me.

I grasped my trembling thighs. "Oh fuck!"

"Is there a problem? Trouble?"

I put my hands on my hips and peered over my shoulder. "Nope. No problem at all. Enjoy the show." I sashayed into the kitchen, gliding my hands over my ass, fully aware of the anguishing ache in my groin.

"Careful, Miss Kelly. You're touching what's mine.

With a flip of my hair, I bent over to pick up Derek's clothes from the kitchen floor and the egg buzzed and hummed. He left it on a little too long, my knees buckled and I landed on my damp bathrobe. I writhed and whimpered with my ass in the air.

Derek caught me slipping a hand between my legs. "I can see you, young lady. Don't you dare touch yourself."

He flipped it off. I flipped him off and stood up. He laughed. "Nice. Very ladylike."

I collected myself, and the wet clothes. "I'm sure the pilgrims would approve. I should take these upstairs to the laundry room."

Derek stopped me. "I don't think so. I'm not letting you out of my sight."

"Somebody should take them upstairs. Do you want to come with me?"

A devilish gleam flashed in his eyes. "I have an idea."

Once again, he put my naked butt on the island. He grabbed the *Saran Wrap* and ripped off a long sheet. He rolled it into a strip and bound my wrists. "Since you misbehaved earlier you'll have to stay like this until I get back. My baby, what do you think of this little game?"

"Honestly, I envisioned me coming a whole lot more…so…"

He leaned forward and whispered in my ear, "Good girls get rewarded instantly. Bad girls get it the hard way. Tell me what you want, Nia."

His hot, sweet breath on my neck made me shudder. I exhaled. "I want it the hard way."

"Hmm…then I'm sure you'll come up with something." His lips brushed along my collarbone. "Be right back."

Me and my pussy were helpless for now, but the wheels were turning for getting it the hard way. I contemplated my next move.

Molly came in with her tail going a mile a minute. "What's a matter, girl? Do you miss Coco and Sammy?" Julia and Phillip chartered a plane to fly to California, so they could take the dogs with them.

Molly cocked her head at me. "Yes, Molly. Mommy is naked with *Saran Wrap* around her wrists. It's how I roll." She trotted off snatching her bright blue dinosaur toy. No doubt, she was heading to her hoarder tree.

Derek returned to the kitchen. I drank him in with my eyes. His long muscled frame, perfect ass, and broad shoulders were the most flawless things I'd ever laid eyes on, not to mention his horn of plenty and sack so venti.

"What's that look for? Are you dreaming up a naughty scheme?"

"No, Mr. Pierce, I'm just checking you out all naked in the kitchen. I like it."

He closed in on me and ran his hand up my inner thigh. "I like what I see too. You have the softest skin, and the most gorgeous body." His lips graced mine with a sublime, sweet kiss that flushed me from root to tip. "You're beautiful." He cupped my breasts. "I kind of enjoy you like this. Bound and at my mercy."

"I kind of enjoy it too. Just promise me one thing. Don't ever shove anything into my mouth, but your cock. I like to talk."

He laughed and taunted. "Really? I hadn't noticed. Maybe I should keep you like this and feed you Thanksgiving dinner."

"You could, if you knew how to cook. The chef needs to baste her bird. I'll baste yours later."

"Sounds like an excellent idea." He cut the *Saran Wrap* off my wrists and massaged them. "Okay, my little chef, the kitchen is all yours." He picked up the remote and sat at the table, glued to my every move.

As soon as I bent over to tend to the turkey, he hit the remote. When I stood up, he switched it off. It was his pattern. Every time my butt was in the air, the buzz rocked my walls. It was like being shaken not stirred. I was so wrung out from going to the edge and not coming. The build up and weight of the egg grew painful. There was only one thing to do. I bent over and shoved my ass in Derek's face. I had no plans of standing up until I got relief.

He patted my bottom and stood me up. "Nice try. Always looking for trouble."

I straddled his lap. "Derek, please. If you think about it, I've been good and bad. Don't you think I should be rewarded instantly, the hard way."

"That's an interesting way of putting it."

Molly ran in with a tennis ball in her mouth. She threw it on the floor and barked. That was her way of saying, play with me. I was so desperate for Derek to play with me, I didn't know what to do. Or did I?

"Aw, Derek, she misses Coco and Sammy. Maybe you should put some shorts on and play with her for a bit. I need to do some more food prep anyway."

"I don't know. Do I dare leave you alone for a second?"

"Oh I dare you."

I hopped off him and his hand slipped between my legs. "You are so wet. For your sake I hope you'll be good."

He picked up the tennis ball. "Come on, Molly. A quick game of fetch."

I shouted after them. "Hey, aren't you forgetting something? You're naked."

"So? The entire street went out of town. I'm embracing Naked Thanksgiving."

"Well, be careful. Molly gets a little wild. I don't want anything to happen to your Plymouth Cock."

They ran outside and I fled to the bathroom. With all the pressure from the egg, I had to pee something fierce. I wasn't supposed to but I removed the egg of misery. What a relief!

I ran a warm washcloth over my aching bits. There was no way I was putting it back in. If I was going to get it the hard way, I was going to make it count. I cleaned the egg with a tad of soap and warm water and took it with me to the kitchen. I proudly displayed it right next to the bottle of olive oil on the island.

I glanced out the window and caught a glimpse of naked Derek and Molly frolicking in the backyard. Sure enough, the bright blue dinosaur was peering out from under the hoarder tree. After one more spectacular catch, Molly sped toward the house and Derek followed. Just what would happen when he spied the extracted buzz yolk?

"All done?" I asked as Molly dove into her water bowl.

"Yes. And Plymouth Cock is ready to settle

somewhere," Derek joked.

I bent over the island with my chin resting on my hands. "My territory's been ready since the turn of the century."

Derek clicked the remote and nothing happened. He arched his eyebrow and approached the island while I shot him an expression that was as innocent as a cherub.

His eyes widened when he spotted the egg. "Nia Kelly, you fucking didn't."

I licked my lips. "Derek Pierce, I fucking did."

He stalked behind me and pressed a hand on my back. "How convenient you're already bent over the island. I distinctly remember saying only I could remove Lacey's gift. Do you remember that?"

I clutched the countertop in sheer jubilation for my punishment. The stinging clap of Derek's hand across my ass was what I craved all day. "Yes. And I willfully disobeyed you. I need to be disciplined."

His fingers skimmed my bottom and my pussy snapped, crackled, and popped like a bowl of Rice Crispies. "Open your legs and brace yourself, Nia. I'm going to spank you, the hard way."

I obeyed, while all my muscles below the waist clenched and twitched. The first spank landed right in the middle. It was like a three for one. He hit both cheeks and my crack with blunt force.

I gasped. "Oh fuck."

He caressed my cheeks. "Oh fuck, is right. You

played with fire and your ass is about to get burned."

Each cheek absorbed another crack of his hand, and my unruly fluids gushed and dripped down my legs. After three more blows he stopped, spread me open and blew another stream of cool air on my sex.

A tremor quaked within. "Oh God, Derek, please. Please touch me. Please, I'm going crazy."

He lightly grazed along my slit with his oak-like wood. "I would love to reward you instantly, if you had been good. What were you, Nia?"

I wriggled, trying to suck his cock inside me. "I was bad. I've been bad all day. I'm a bad, bad girl."

He gripped my hips and pulled his goody stick away. "That's right. You may need to eat Thanksgiving dinner standing up when I'm done with you."

He resumed his harsh spanks with the skill of an expert. My nerve endings were fried and fused at the same time. He reduced me to a mass of pulping flesh. My ass burned like an inferno. Each contact it had with Derek's hand produced a squishing stream of powerful squirts.

Without warning, he bulldozed his massive length inside me in one jarring thrust.

"Ahhh…yes. Fuck me. Oh my God."

My fluttering cunt gobbled up his strapping cock, basting him in my juices. One hand splayed on my back holding me firmly in place and his other smacked my right cheek, while he supplied me with dynamic, full-fuck strokes.

He pulled out halfway and slowed. "Your punishment isn't quite over. Give me that bottle of olive oil."

Oh shit! What was he going to do? Toss my salad? I handed him the bottle and both of his hands released me, but he continued his easy rocks of my hole.

Spreading my cheeks, he dabbed the olive oil on my anus. "Your ass needs more training. When I fuck you here, you're getting all of it, all the way to my balls. Understand?"

"Oh God, yes. I want it. I want all of it." It was all I could do not to ask him to take me there right now. Ass play on turkey day was *o-fucking-kay!*

"That's a good girl." He roved his hands over my back with tenderness. "I'm going to push you, baby. I need to see what you can take. Use your safe word if you have to."

"Okay. I'm ready."

Derek took his time ramping us back up into a luscious pace of pleasure. His first finger slid in easy, eliciting murmurs of passion. I loved to be filled up like this. To be tested to see how much could I take. The second finger crammed its way in and I shrieked at its encroachment. He drilled both holes with shafting precision, skillfully propelling me to the cliff of a cataclysmic climax. Derek calmed the tunneling of my ass. His fingers split and stretched me open, preparing me.

A third errant digit wedged inside, stealing all of

the air from my lungs. "Oh Jesus!"

He stilled. "Are you okay, sweetie?"

"Yes. Oh God. I'm close. It's so fucking good."

"That's it, baby. You take it. You take it all for me."

He submerged his cock and fingers, ramming me full throttle. It was a fucking like no other. He filled and stuffed me beyond measure. The way his fingers and cock drove so deep, pushing me beyond blessed delirium, with the Holy Grail of pumping power. With one final lethal thrust, he blasted me to obliteration, causing a tsunami of orgasms, one crashing into the other. Derek's outpouring eruption of cum ruptured inside me as we drained each other of every delicious tidbit.

His body fell atop of mine. The warmth of his skin was intoxicating. What was wrong with me? I couldn't possibly still be horny. Could I?

I glowed, relishing the feel of his heavy breath cascading over me. "That was amazing."

He trailed soft kisses down my back. "You're what's amazing. Sweetie, look at me."

I angled my face to meet his gaze. "Nia, my angel, on our wedding night when I claim you fully, its going to be incredible for both of us. You feel ready and I can't wait to be inside you."

"I can't wait either. I almost begged you to, but I didn't want to…"

"Change the plan."

I giggled. "You know me too well."

He grinned. "I do, Miss Kelly, I do. Now, stay right there. Don't move."

He washed his hands and cleansed me with a warm paper towel. "I better put you in the tub. The olive oil isn't really…hmm… I might have used too much."

"That's okay. I give you mad props for your improvisational skills."

He bent down and kissed my forehead. "You're always game for anything. I love it. I love you."

When he stood up his half-hard dick was at my mouth. "I love you. And your cock and I are besties." I peered up at him. "Thank you for cleaning me up. I think I should return the favor." The flat of my tongue licked the underside of his velvety flesh. The sweet and salty savory tang of our cum hit my taste buds as they merged together in my mouth. I suckled his tip inside, and he hissed and swelled under my cunning cock sucking abilities. I bobbed up and down his veined shaft, feasting on a yummy mouthful of hardening maleness.

"Hey, sweetie. Come here." He pulled out of my mouth and sat me upright. "There's some place I always wanted to make love to you, and I think today would be perfect."

"Where?"

He smoothed the hair off my face. "On the balcony upstairs. It's a beautiful day, and not a soul around. You can announce your arrival as loud as you want."

I flung my arms around his neck. "I've wanted to do it there since the first morning I woke up in this house."

He rested his forehead on mine. "I have to have you." He hoisted me off the island. "Let's go upstairs. I need to feel you again, baby."

Derek flew upstairs and out the open patio doors. My love and desire for him consumed me as he worshiped me with his mouth. He eased into a chair with me astride him while his lips explored my taut nipples. My breasts budded with pink, rousing a melting sweetness within me. His mouth made a path to mine. Our kiss amplified as his hands slid down my waist, and massaged my ass. The scent of sex in the air fueled our fiery passion.

"Take me, Nia. Put me inside you."

I lightly grasped his cock and guided it inside. My slick walls encased his rock-iron erection. I circled my hips, grinding in a slow, sultry motion.

"That's it, baby. Nice and slow. It's just you and me. The rest of the world doesn't exist."

I exhaled in joy. "Yes. We're in our bubble."

A tender smile crossed his face. "Our bubble?"

I pressed my palms into his chest, rolling up and down his length. "When we're like this. I call it being in our bubble. It's the only time I feel safe and protected. No one can hurt us."

He clutched me to his chest. "My sweet girl, when you're scared, hold onto to me tighter. Remember, I'll be strong enough for both of us. Nothing can touch us. I won't let it."

I held onto to him with all my might, our bodies swaying as one. "You won't ever let go?"

"Never. You and me, always and forever. I'm going to marry you, Nia Kelly, and love you for the rest of your life."

I lifted my head and our eyes locked on one another. "I'm going to marry you, Derek Pierce, and drive you crazy for the rest of your life."

His blue eyes sparkled brighter than the sun shining down on us. "I would expect nothing less from my girl... God you feel good. I love watching you fuck me."

I accelerated our pace. "I wasn't aware we were fucking. I thought we were making love."

"With you, naughty Nia, there's always a little fucking going on. I wouldn't have it any other way."

"Well, in that case." I eased almost all of the way out of him and slammed my pussy to his base. We let out a low groan and found a tempo that bound our bodies together in salacious ecstasy. Even though we were fucking, our love for each other flowed like warm honey, and our connection soared to the ends of the earth.

His hands clasped my back and bottom as he lifted me out of the chair. "Wrap your legs around me, sweetie."

I coiled my legs around him and he carried me to

the patio doors. He shut them tight and pressed my back into the glass. "Do you want it the hard way again, Nia?"

"Yes. Give it to me."

He plunged into me even deeper, with a series of walloping strokes. I already had a load of Derek's creamy seed buried inside and was hungry for more. My limitless appetite for him, and for this, this soul-drenching cosmic force of Derek and me, was all I ever longed for.

He took my mind and body on a journey to a different time and space. I could get lost in him and in us. There was no fear, nothing weighing us down. It was liberating to give up all control. His love allowed me to trust him to bring me to new heights, while testing my limits. It surpassed anything I thought was ever possible.

With my back skidding against the glass panel, Derek forged ahead with a countless multitude of dominant thrusts. Each one commanded a rippling tide of wonder inside me. We were swimming in a torrential flood of my juices, spiraling to the fringe of fuck mania.

Derek clasped my chin. "I want to hear you, Nia. Tell me when you're coming. I want you to scream for me."

I heaved. "Yes…ah…yes."

He launched into me, delivering a ripping kill shot to my cunt that tore me to pieces.

"I'm coming! Oh Jesus, fuck, I'm coming!"

This shattering, fierce sensation wrenched my body and transported me to the wonderland of orgasms.

Derek growled. "Fuck...fuck yes!" His cum rocketed inside me like a missile of lush syrup.

Time stood still as he peeled me off the door and cradled my body against his until the last flickers of our climax subsided.

With exhausted limbs, Derek reclined back into the chair and held me tight. His large hands caressed the back of my head and the small of my back. We were quiet until a soft breeze washed over us and I shivered.

"Are you cold, sweetie? I should probably get you inside and into a warm bath."

I nestled my cheek into his chest. "That sounds like heaven."

"You're heaven. You're my heaven on earth." He rocked me gently. "I like being in our bubble. That's a perfect way to describe it."

"Yep. The bubble is the bomb."

"Yes it is." My skin broke out in goose bumps. "Okay. Bath time."

We disengaged our sticky, satisfied bodies and went to the door. Derek grabbed the knob. It didn't budge. "Oh shit. Were locked out."

"Derek, please be joking."

"I wish I was."

"What are we going to do? I don't think Molly is well trained enough to come open the door."

"Hang on. I'll think of something."

"We are so screwed."

Derek glanced over the side of the balcony. "No. I can climb down there. The other doors are open. It'll be fine."

I checked the distance to the ground. "Are you sure? That's quite a drop."

He kissed the top of my head. "I'm sure it'll be okay."

"All right. Be careful. Don't hurt any of the good stuff."

He bounded over the side of the balcony with the ease of a super hero. Once he landed safely, I breathed a sigh of relief.

The sun set early these days and a slight chill filled the air. I took in the beautiful view and looked to see if Molly was still playing. She wasn't. It was then I noticed her bright blue dinosaur wasn't by her hoarder tree. Hmm…maybe she brought it inside, but she never does that. A crackling noise sounded in the yard and I jumped. I could have sworn I saw someone by the back left corner of the property. My heart sunk to my stomach. *Is someone out there?*

I pounded on the patio doors. "Derek. Derek, where are you?"

He flung open the doors and I clung to him. "Hey. What's all this? You're shaking."

"I think someone is out there. I saw something… I think…I don't know…I'm not sure."

"Stay here. I'll take a look."

"Let me go with you."

He grasped my shoulders. "No. I forbid it. Stay put."

He cautiously made his way out onto the balcony. I couldn't take it. I had to see for myself.

I pointed to the suspicious spot. "The noise I heard came from over there."

"Nia, I told you to stay inside. I got this."

"But I wanted to tell you…"

He raised his voice. "Inside. Now."

I stomped off. He came back inside and locked the doors. "I didn't see anything. I'm going to head downstairs, make sure everything is locked and turn on the alarm."

"Are you mad at me?"

He wrapped me up in his arms. "No angel. Just get in the tub for me. I'll bring you a glass of wine."

I arched up on my tiptoes and kissed his cheek. "Okay. When you're downstairs, can you look for Molly's blue dinosaur?"

"Sure. Why?"

"I can't tell you right now. I have strict orders to get in the tub."

"That's my girl."

Derek was right. A warm bath was exactly what I needed to soothe my worked over flesh.

He returned to the bathroom with wine and Molly in tow. "I didn't find her dinosaur."

"That's weird."

Derek climbed in the tub. "What's weird?"

"Earlier today she took it outside. I saw it just under her hoarder tree and it's not there now. Do you think someone really was in our backyard today?"

"No. Molly could have done anything with that toy. Once we give them to her they are lost causes."

I peeked over the side of the tub at Molly demolishing another one. "You're probably right. That monkey doesn't stand a chance. Maybe I was seeing things."

"I'm thinking maybe we've gotten a little too comfortable since nothing strange has happened lately. I'm looking at today's little scare as a wake-up call."

"What do you mean?"

"I always believed if Larry Wall was going to come after you, he would've done it by now. It seems with Walter and Brooke out of our lives the threat disappeared. But the truth is, it hasn't. We need to be more diligent about keeping you safe and protected. It was careless of us to leave the doors open."

"I guess we got carried away with Naked Thanksgiving."

"Which is now a tradition we should always honor."

I crawled onto his lap and the water splashed around us. "I like creating traditions and making memories."

"I do too, sweetie. We'll have a lifetime of them. I would like to start a new tradition after we get out of the tub. It's a surprise. Actually I have two surprises for you."

I was as giddy as child. "You do? Can we get out of the tub now? I can't wait."

"Of course. Whatever my girl wants."

I popped up out of the water. "Did you hear that, Molly? He said whatever I want. You're my witness.

"Very cute, young lady. Dry off and go lay on the bed. On your tummy."

I squealed and dried myself at breakneck speed. Then I flattened on my belly and waited for Derek.

He sat on the bed with the lavender lotion in hand. "How's your bottom, sweetie? Are you sore from your spanking?"

"Everything is a good sore. You don't ever have to worry. My ass has a high pain tolerance, my boobs, not so much."

He chuckled and rubbed the lotion over my bum. "You never cease to amaze with the way your body responds. I love it." His lips brushed my shoulder. "There. All done."

I rolled to my side. "So what's this surprise you're springing on me? I mean, I'm already naked. What more could you want?"

"Sit tight. You'll see." He went to the closet and retrieved a silver package with a green bow.

"It's not Christmas. It's Thanksgiving?"

"I know. Indulge me and open it."

I ripped open the package with zeal. It was a soft

green pair of Christmas pajamas with little candy canes. "Derek, they're so cute. I love them. Wait. Do you want me to put clothes on?"

"Well, you looked so cute in the ones Julia got you. I was going to start a new tradition."

"Like Pajama Thanksgiving?"

He grinned. "Yeah. Something like that. But naked works too."

"Can we have both? Naked during the day and snuggly PJs at night. Once I turn off the oven, it won't be so hot in the house."

"That sounds like a plan."

"What about my other surprise?"

"That will have to wait until after dinner."

"In that case, I better get back to the kitchen."

* * * *

"Everything smells so good, sweetie."

"Thank you." I sauntered over to him in my new candy cane pajamas and snaked my arms around his waist. "We should be ready to eat in twenty minutes. The turkey just needs to sit and cool a little while longer."

He kissed my forehead. "Ah, yes. So the juices can redistribute."

"Yes. You remembered."

"I've never forgotten anything about juices."

"Me neither. Do you care if I call Aunt Mary Jane

before we eat? I won't be long."

"No, of course not. Go call her. Your phone is upstairs."

I gave him a quick peck and when I looked into his eyes, I saw something I've never seen before. "Derek, what's wrong? You look, sad or something."

"No. I'm not. I...I was just thinking I left my phone upstairs too, because for once no one needs to get in touch with me. *First Bite* is over and I don't start working on *The Alec Stone Chronicles* until the spring. I don't know, it feels weird, but I'm not sad. I don't know what to call it."

"You know what I call it? A happy holiday."

"You're right. Just for a second I thought I would miss the rat race. But, I'm fine. Go call Aunt Mary Jane and Uncle Bill. Tell them I said Happy Thanksgiving."

"Okay. I'll be right back. Pour a glass of wine and watch some football. If you want, we can eat dinner in front of the TV. I love football."

"You love football?"

"Hell yes! You have so much left to discover about me, Mr. Pierce."

I bopped up the stairs, grabbed my phone and dialed Aunt Mary Jane and Uncle Bill. "Happy Thanksgiving."

"Happy Thanksgiving. Did you and Derek eat yet?"

"No, we will in a bit. I called you earlier, but I guess you took off to your neighbors already. Where did you go?"

"Oh, we went to the Bensons' and ate with our church friends."

"The Bensons? Didn't you call Ann Benson an old bag? I didn't think you liked her."

"Well, she annoys the crap out of me, but Bill likes her fucking sweet potato casserole, so what the hell. I just drink a lot of wine and smile."

I cracked up. "You don't like the casserole?"

"No, it tastes like hammered shit."

I fell back on the bed, laughing hysterically. Aunt Mary Jane with wine in her was even more hilarious than usual. "Oh God. Hammered shit. That's a new one."

She snickered too. "Well, you know what I mean. For fuck sake, it's just some marshmallows and cinnamon. You should hear your Uncle Bill go on about it."

"Is he awake? I'd like to say Happy Thanksgiving to him too."

"No. He fell asleep watching football. I'll tell him you called. Is the wedding still on? How's Derek?"

"Yes, very funny. It's still on. Derek's...well...I don't know. It's probably nothing, but right before I called you he said he thought he missed the rat race. Do you think LA will still have a hold on him after he's starts shooting his new series in Vegas?"

"No. But it's a big change, and men don't handle change as well as women do."

"I don't handle change well at all."

"Yes you do. You just don't like it. There's a difference. At least you recognize it and talk about it. Just be there for him and love him."

"That sounds like something Mom would say."

"That is something your mom did say when we moved to Kansas. It was good advice."

"Well, you were definitely right about one thing. Men do bring a knife to a gunfight. I spilled my bottle of water on the floor and Derek handed my one damn paper towel."

She chuckled. "If he ever hands you two consider it a fucking miracle."

"I love it when drop the f-bomb. You just made my Thanksgiving. I love you."

"I love you, Nia."

* * * *

"Nia, this is delicious. This is best Thanksgiving meal I've ever had."

"Now I know you're just being nice. You've probably had Thanksgiving dinner prepared by world-class chefs."

"That's true and hands down, yours is better."

"But I made it all super healthy, except for the cheesy corn."

"And it's delicious." He grasped my hand. "Thank you, my sweet girl. This has been the best

Thanksgiving of my life."

"Mine too. Thank you for making memories with me. I love you."

"I love you too." He rose from the table and kissed my temple. "Since you cooked, I'll clean up."

He looked around the kitchen and was like a lost child who couldn't find their mother. Poor, privileged Derek didn't have a clue. "Honey, do you even know how to clean? Don't you have people for that?"

"Settle down, young lady. Of course I can clean. I just need to know where you keep the...those plastic container things."

"You mean *Tupperware*? It's in that cabinet next to the dishwasher." I was enjoying the show, wondering how long it would be before he admitted defeat. The insides of my cabinets were meticulous and organized. Somehow, Derek managed to pull out one container and the rest tumbled on the floor. I stifled a snicker.

"You think this is funny, don't you?"

I crinkled my nose. "A little. Are you sure you don't need any help?"

"No. I'm good.'

After burning his finger on the *Crock-Pot*, he unplugged it, and moved on to the Brussels Sprouts. Armed with *Tupperware* he scooped them into the container with ease. Brimming with confidence, he plopped the *Pyrex* glassware into the dishwasher without rinsing it.

"Wow!" I exclaimed. "That is so gangster."

He arched his eyebrow. "What is?"

"You. You just threw that dish in there without rinsing. You're like a cleaning renegade."

"Are you supposed to rinse it first? I thought that was the dishwasher's job."

"Well, it helps."

He picked up the turkey baster, and made a trail of turkey juice from the stove to the sink. The control freak in me nearly had a heart attack, but I approached the situation delicately.

"Derek, honey, can I please help?"

He conceded with a sweet smile. "Okay. I'm probably making you nuts."

I got up from the table and wrapped my arms around his waist. "Yes. You are. But thanks for trying. I love to clean. I can get this all put away in five minutes. I don't mind. I want to do it."

He embraced me. "In other words, you want me to get out of your way."

"Well, I would never say it like that, but yes."

His lips touched my forehead. "Then I'll leave you to it. I'll go upstairs and get your second surprise."

"That sounds perfect."

As predicted, within five minutes the kitchen was spotless, including the floor. Derek returned to the kitchen with a huge grin on his face. Just what was he up to?

"Is that my surprise behind your back?"

"Yes."

"Is it a doozie?"

"It is indeed. You may need to sit down for this, sweetie."

I hopped up on the island, excited with anticipation.

"Close you eyes for me."

I squeezed them shut, with my heart pounding.

"Okay, open them."

I peered down in astonishment. It was the Bulgari Corona tennis necklace, with too many diamonds to count. I gasped. "Oh, Derek. It's...I don't know what to say... It's too beautiful for words. It's—"

"Please don't say it's too much. I picked it out myself, especially for you. I'd like you to wear it when you marry me."

Tears spilled down my cheeks. I glanced up and him and nodded.

He wiped them away with the pad of his thumb. "Hey, I hope these are happy tears."

"Yes. I'm so happy. You're...you're... I love you."

His mouth came down on mine and he graced my lips with the softest of kisses. "I love you too. Would you like to try it on?"

"Is it bad luck, since it's for the wedding?"

"I think that's only your dress."

"Which I still have to get."

"Perfect. I think we can risk a little sneak peek of the necklace. May I?"

"Yes. Please."

Derek put this extraordinary piece around my neck. I instantly felt like royalty, even if I was wearing candy cane pajamas. "It's flawless, my angel. It's just like you."

"I have to go see." I hopped off the island and made a beeline for the mirror in the hallway off the kitchen. This was by far the most exquisite piece Derek had ever given me, and the most expensive. I ran back to the kitchen and jumped into his arms. "I love it. I wish Christmas Eve was tomorrow. I can't wait to get married."

"If Christmas Eve was tomorrow, you'd be getting married in diamonds and PJs. Hey, that could be part of our Thanksgiving tradition. First we're naked then in pajamas, and I shower you with diamonds."

"Well, if you insist."

"I insist. I insist, on spoiling you. Any arguments?"

"Not a one…for now."

"That's my girl. Now, what would you like to do?"

"It might sound kind of silly, but last year after dinner at Julia's we binge watched Thanksgiving episodes of *Friends*. Would that be okay?"

He sat me down. "Of course. You find your show and I'll get us some wine."

We cuddled up with Molly on the couch. When the bell rang, I jerked up off the sofa. "Who could that be? It's after nine."

Derek got up. "I'll go. You stay here. Remember, we aren't taking any chances."

With cautious steps, Derek inched his way to the door. "Hey, it's Shannon."

"Shannon? Well, let her in. Maybe something's wrong."

When Derek opened the door, the alarm went off. He punched in the code and they made their way to the kitchen.

"Hey, happy Thanksgiving," I said as I embraced her. "What's going on?"

She looked at me with puffy red eyes. "Oh nothing. I worked today and it was real quiet at the club...and... I don't know."

"Have you been crying?"

"A little. I guess, I just feel alone. The holidays aren't much fun when you have no one to spend them with."

"Do you want to have a glass of wine with us and watch TV?"

"No. I'm sorry. I shouldn't have come."

"Shannon, you're welcome to stay," Derek interjected.

"Yeah. Are you hungry? We have tons of leftovers."

"No, the chef from the club brought me over a plate. So, I'm good. I think I just needed to see a friend. Oh my God." She gasped. "Your necklace, it's so beautiful."

"Oh...thanks." I ran my fingertips over the diamonds, still in shock that they were really around my neck. "Derek just gave it to me. I'm going to wear it on my wedding day… And I feel like an asshole for telling you that. I'm sorry."

"No. Don't be. I'm so happy for you." Her behavior turned skittish. "You know, I feel kind of silly now that I'm here. I'm going to go."

"Are you sure?" I asked.

"Yeah." She hurried to the door. "Happy Thanksgiving. I'll see you tomorrow."

* * * *

Later that night in bed, before Derek turned the light out, he turned on his phone and checked it. "It's kind of late. Why are you checking your phone?"

He placed it on the nightstand. "You're right. Force of habit I guess."

"Derek, are you sure you made the right decision, to do the new show here?"

"Yes. Of course. It's just that, I used to think of Vegas as my escape from LA, and now I find myself not having anything to escape from. Does that make sense?"

"Yes. Aunt Mary Jane told me that men don't handle change well."

"But I'm excited about the changes, the show, and most importantly marrying you."

"It's still a lot. Plus, *First Bite* was such a big part of your life. It would only be natural for you to feel a let down after that."

"Since when did you get so smart?"

"Since Aunt Mary Jane gave me some good advice. She said just to love you and be there for you."

"Actually, I think you're both pretty smart. I like that advice. Come here."

I nestled into my regular spot and sighed. "I can't stop thinking about Shannon, how sad she was, and the way she left so suddenly. I mean, her moods have always been a little eratic, especially since Walter left town, but tonight was different. I felt awful for her."

Derek played with my hair. "I know. She's a good friend."

"I never told you this, but that first night we hung out, she confided in me that both of her parents had passed away too. She's an only child, so she doesn't have any family. I keep thinking that could easily be me. All alone on Thanksgiving, without any family."

"Baby, you never have to worry about that. I'm your family. I'm going to be your husband. You, me, and Molly are family forever and always.

"And I'm yours. I love you."

"I love you too. Goodnight, my sweet girl."

Chapter Twelve

The next morning, the loud vibration of Derek's phone on the nightstand shook us out of a deep sleep.

"Sorry, baby. I forgot to turn it off last night."

Still groggy, I asked, "Who's calling this early? Maybe you should answer. It might be important."

"It's Keith. Hey, man, what's up?"

After a long pause, Derek's sprang out of the bed and paced the floor. "You're kidding? No, I wouldn't have any idea." His eyes focused on me. "They can't possibly think that. Okay…okay…yes… I'll get to the bottom of it. I'm sorry I'm not there to help you deal with the fallout… Yep, keep me posted."

"Honey, what's wrong?"

"It's Eden. Someone in her inner circle leaked her secret. The whole world knows she's gay. She's out of the closet, and not on her own terms. This is bad."

Derek flicked on the TV and it was breaking news on every morning program. The media packed around the guarded gates of her home. According to the news report, endorsement deals hung in the balance, and so was her upcoming role as the new Bond girl. It saddened me this was still such a big deal in this day and age.

"Oh you're right. Poor Eden. Is there anything we

can do?"

"They're trying to find out who leaked it. So, I have to ask, Nia, did you ever tell anyone Eden is gay?"

My body flushed in furious shock. "What? Are you really accusing me? I would never, ever say anything."

Tension filled his face. "I know you wouldn't do it on purpose, but by accident did you let it slip? Maybe you said something to Brooke while we were broken up. She could've gone to the press, since you've had a falling out."

I hauled myself out of bed and met his suspicion with fire in my eyes. "No. I told you I never said anything. I think you better drop it."

He gripped my shoulders. "I'm trying to help them figure it out."

"By accusing me? That's such bullshit."

"Nia, you don't get it. If you told anyone, then I'm to blame for Eden's nightmare. I'm the one who asked her to trust you in the first place."

I shrugged him off. "And now you're acting like you don't trust me. Seriously, let it go. I didn't do anything, and at the end of the day this is not our problem."

"Eden's career could be over. I'm just trying to help her."

"By pissing me off? Because that's what you're doing by questioning my integrity. I mean, did you hear what they just said on TV. She's holding a press conference. It's out. There's nothing anyone can do.

Her fans will probably rally around her and this could be the best thing that ever happened to her. She doesn't have to hide who she really is anymore. On some level I'm sure she's relieved."

He rubbed the back of his neck. "So, you're saying there's not even a small chance this could've been leaked by you. I have to know."

"Are you fucking kidding me? Did you not listen to one word I just said?" I stormed toward the bathroom. "I'm taking a shower, and when I get out, this conversation needs to be over."

My cell phone beeped. "Damn it. I better see who it is. It might be someone from the club." I marched to the nightstand to get my phone, and Derek stopped me dead in my tracks.

"Nia, your phone."

"What about it?"

"Give me your phone."

"Fine. It was just a text from Julia. Here." I handed it to him.

He scrolled through. "I knew it. The text I sent you the night I was at Eden and Heather's, you never deleted from your phone. Isn't that the night you were out with the girls, dancing on the bar? Answer me."

"Yes. But I don't think—"

He interrupted in a fury. "Great! Because of your irresponsibility, someone could've seen this text. I told you it was unacceptable to leave your phone unattended and unlocked. Once again, you and your fucking phone."

The rage inside had me had nowhere to go, so I unleashed it on Derek. "You know what, you and Hollywood, and your friends can all go fuck themselves. I'm done." I ripped my phone from his hands and pushed past him.

He grabbed my arm. "Stop right there. We are not done. I'm trying to get to the bottom of this."

"At what cost? When you came to Vegas to win me back you said you realized you needed to put me first. Look at what you're doing. You're not putting me first. You're putting me on trial for something I didn't do."

"Okay. You've made your point, but don't you understand, your careless behavior with your phone could ruin Eden."

I threw my phone on the bed. "I'm so fucking sick of you scolding me like a child. Do you know what it's like for me to try to fit into your world? It sucks! I can't ever do anything right. I will never be good enough for you. I'm so sick of beating myself up trying." The anger and hurt ripped me open like a bullet to the heart.

He softened somewhat. "Don't say you're not good enough for me. That's not what this is about."

"I'll tell you what it's about. It's about you. You need to decide what you really want. I saw it. I saw it in your eyes last night. Our life here isn't enough for you. On some level, you miss that Hollywood machine of drama and one crisis after another."

"That's not true."

"Isn't it? One phone call from Keith and you're a different person. Someone I don't want to live with."

"What are you saying?"

"I'm saying you should go. You should go back to LA and think long and hard about us."

"Nia, I'm not going anywhere. Look, I'm sorry. This mess with Eden caught me off guard. I don't want to leave you. Not after yesterday." His hand cupped my face. "Our first Thanksgiving together was incredible. Please, sweetie. Let's forget about all of this and go back to our bubble."

I took his hand away from my face and backed up. "I can't do that. Not after you accused me over and over of betraying Eden's trust. That's not who I am. And you should know that. Everything you said to me this morning erased yesterday for me. It's like it didn't mean anything to you."

"That's not true. I...I don't know. Maybe something is going on with me that I don't understand."

It felt like someone took a vice grip to my heart. I squeezed my eyes shut unable to squelch my tears. "Then you need to go."

He yanked me to him, holding me to his chest. "Please. Forgive me. Let's forget this and move on. I don't want to go."

I broke down. "I want to forgive you, but I can't live like this. I don't belong in your world. I don't think I belong anywhere."

"Baby, of course you belong. You belong to me.

I'm yours and you are mine."

"I don't know if I believe in that anymore."

"Then I'll believe for both us. What do I have to do to make this right?"

I released myself from Derek's arms. "It's what I have to do. I have to let you go."

I turned to head to the bathroom and Derek's phone vibrated. I snapped my head around and caught him reaching for it. "Sorry. I have to take it. It's Eden."

"Go ahead. Answer it. Just be gone when I get out of the shower."

* * * *

"So, you haven't talked to him at all?" Lacey asked.

It was three days after the disastrous blow up with Derek and me. Lacey was in my office at the club.

"No. Not one word. He texts me every night and says he loves me, and I text it back. It's so weird. I'm in limbo. I don't even know if we're getting married. I'm glad you and Jake decided to go to Hawaii for Christmas. There might not be a wedding."

"Do you still want to marry him?"

"Of course I do, but the ball is in his court. He has to decide what he wants. He made me believe he wanted a quieter life here. Now I don't know. I'm starting to lose hope. Maybe love just isn't enough."

"Do you regret getting back together?"

"In some ways I do. I hate feeling like this. I mean, you only see charming, sweet Derek. There's this whole other side. I call it LA Derek. When he rears his head, it makes me question everything."

"I'm sorry, Nia. I can't imagine him being harsh with you for a moment. I've never seen any man more in love than Derek."

"Except for maybe Jake."

Her face flushed. "Well, he's not into PDA, but in private…"

"Oh my God. I've never seen you blush. But I've heard you, um, agreeing with him very loud and enthusiastically at night."

Lacey covered her face. "You heard us having sex?"

"No. I just heard *you*."

"Oh God…sorry."

"Don't apologize. I'm the one who's sorry. Because I told Derek to go back to LA, you guys have to stay with me and lose your privacy."

"That's okay. We would both worry about you staying alone. I don't know how you deal with it. I've never met Larry Wall, but he sounds like such an asshole, and now you have to live in constant fear."

"It's awful. I wonder sometimes if my life will ever be normal. Will I ever be able to be alone again? You and Jake might be stuck with me for life."

"That would be fine with me, unless you want to do a three-way like Christa. I'm not sharing."

I laughed. "You're safe with me. Oh, and speaking of Christa, she gave her two-week notice and I cut her a check and let her go. We don't need her anyway. Around the holidays everyone abandons their workout routines."

"Everyone but you and me. We're gym rats for life."

"Truer words were never spoken. These days it's my sanctuary. When things get crazy, I know without a doubt I will feel better after a workout."

"Yep. For sure." Lacey rose from her chair. "I'm about to teach a private with Nancy right now. So, I'll catch you later."

"Sounds good. See you tonight."

Lacey turned to leave and stopped. "Nia, I need to tell you something. I don't know how you kept Eden's secret. If I had known she was gay, I probably would've had to tell at least one person. I'm such a blab."

"I guess I always figured it was her secret to tell. Have you been following it? I saw a little blurb on the news, it seems like the support for her is overwhelming."

"Been following? I've been obsessing. I read everything online and Twitter I can find. It looks like someone from Eden's old team spilled the beans. Someone named Aaron. Didn't you know him?"

"Yeah. He used to be Derek's publicist. He was so hot and cold. Kind of strange."

"So, wait. You haven't heard the rumor?"

"No. I'm not on any social media and don't watch TV like I used to."

"After Derek fired him, he pissed off his next client, that girl with the frozen face that's mad all the time, but you can't tell."

"Oh yeah. I can't think of her name."

"I can't either, but, anyway, she fired him too. And he couldn't get any work, so he sold the story to a tabloid for twenty grand."

"Really? Wow…" I slumped back in my chair.

"Nia, what is it?"

"Derek knows it wasn't because I was careless with my phone, and he still hasn't called. Maybe while he's deciding what he wants, he's decided it's not me."

Lacey approached the desk and draped her arm around my shoulder. "That's not true. You two are meant to be. I bet if you called him right now, he'd be back in Vegas in two seconds."

"I can't. Then I won't ever know if he came back because he wanted to or because I asked him to. Maybe our life here just isn't enough for him." I put my head in my hands and fought back the tears.

"Nia, are you all right?" Shannon's voice called from the doorway.

"Yeah. I'm sorry."

"You still haven't talked to Derek?" she asked.

"No," Lacey responded. "Maybe we need to change the subject."

Shannon's voice turned shrill with defensiveness.

"*Sorry.*"

"It's fine," I replied. "Did you need something?"

"I wanted to talk to you, in private."

Lacey strolled toward the door. "I was just leaving. Later."

"Did you and Lacey have another fight?"

Shannon shut the door. "No. But she kind of pissed me off the night of your bachelorette party."

She plopped down in a chair. "I told her that Walter and I had a couple of three-ways with Christa before we left, and she said that I was an idiot for doing that."

"Lacey says it like it is. Looking back, is that what you really wanted?"

"No. I just wanted him, and I know she's entitled to her opinion, but she never gave Walter a chance. Look, I don't want to start anything, but if I were you, I wouldn't trust her."

"Why would you say that?"

"She also told me at your party, she gets jealous sometimes. She thinks Jake has a crush on you."

"That's crazy. No one has a crush on me."

"Are you kidding? Everyone has a crush on you. It's kind of irritating."

I chuckled. "Yeah. Right. I don't even think Derek has a crush on me."

"Oh come on. I bet he'll be back in Vegas by tomorrow."

"I don't think so. Every hour that goes by, I try to prepare myself that we're not getting married. I quit wearing my ring."

"Which one? You have like a hundred."

"I know. All that beautiful jewelry will go to waste. I'll probably never get to wear that necklace he gave me on Thanksgiving. The whole thing is sad. The truth is, I'm not sure I'm over him accusing me of spilling Eden's secret. He didn't just ask me once, he just kept picking at me."

"You really don't think he's coming back anytime soon?"

I exhaled. "Nope. I'm sorry, I didn't mean to go on about myself. What did you want to talk about?"

Her mood changed on a dime. She perked up in the chair with her big toothy grin. "Okay. Brace yourself. I think Walter is going to propose."

Did I just hallucinate? "You think he's going to what, now?"

"I know it sounds crazy. But the day after Thanksgiving he called me, and oh my God, Nia, he said everything I've been waiting for him to say for months."

"Like what exactly?"

"He apologized for leaving the way he did, and he said Christa was a mistake. Now that we've had some time apart, he realized how much he cared about me."

"Is that it?"

"No. Then the next day he sent me flowers, and said he loved me. The day after that he said he really wanted me to come to California for a while, to see if

I'd like to move there to be with him. I told him I couldn't see myself doing that unless we had some kind of real commitment. When I talked to him yesterday, he said he's coming to Vegas, the day after tomorrow. He wants to take me out for a night on the strip. First-class all the way. I can't believe it."

Who could? "Don't you think it's a little sudden?"

"Maybe it is. But what if it isn't? What if he's my chance at happiness? Shouldn't I take that chance?"

The hope in Shannon's eyes gave me a change of heart. "You should. I want you to be happy. And sometimes that means taking a risk. I say go for it."

Her face filled with glee. "Thank you. I'm so excited. There's just one problem."

"What's that?"

"I don't have a thing to wear."

"Well, I can fix that, Cinderella. You can borrow something of mine."

"Oh yeah, right. You're so tiny I'd never fit."

"I bet you would. Plus, I'll raid Julia's closet too. In fact, we could get Julia's hair and makeup person, Vivian, to come over to my house and give you the royal treatment."

"That's so nice, but I don't think I could afford her."

"No. It's my treat. Julia used to do it for me, and I want to do this for you. Sometimes she would hire a team, if we were getting our nails done too, but since it's just you, Vivian will be great. You'll love her."

"I don't know what to say."

"Just say thank you. Getting you ready for Prince Charming is just the thing I need to kick me out of my funk. You're actually doing me a favor."

"Okay. Thank you. Oh no. What are you thinking? I see your wheels turning?"

I laughed. "You know me too well. I was just thinking, Cinderella should have some special jewelry to wear too. Do you want to borrow something?"

"Are you serious? Do you think it would be okay with Derek?"

I shrugged. "Well, Derek isn't here, is he? The hell with him. You can borrow anything you like."

Shannon sprang from her chair, flew around the desk and embraced me. "Thank you. Thank you so much. I promise I'll take good care of it."

"I know you will. And from the sounds of it Walter will take good care of you too."

She broke our hug. "He will. I really believe he's my future."

"Then that's all that matters."

Chapter Thirteen

"Molly! Coco and Sammy are so excited to see you," Julia exclaimed.

Molly and I walked over to Julia's to hang out, while Shannon primped for Prince Charming. The dogs were a whirling dervish of wiggly butts as they greeted each other.

"You'd think they hadn't seen each other in a year," I said, and bent down to love on Coco and Sammy. I treated Sammy to a scratch on his favorite spot around the ears. "Oh, Sammy. Such a good boy. Maybe you should sneak out tonight and sleep at my place."

"Does he still do that?"

"Every once in awhile. I could tell Molly missed them on Thanksgiving. They're like doggie cousins."

Molly and Sammy zoomed out the dog door for a play. Coco stayed glued to Julia.

"Hey, it's wine thirty." Julia announced. "You want some?"

"Well, duh, of course."

We made our way back to the kitchen and Julia poured the wine. "So, how's Cinderella doing?"

"She's a little nervous. Thanks for dropping off some dresses this morning. She picked the low-cut black one."

"Oh good. She'll look great in that. Did you remember to text Jake to tell him you got here okay?"

"No. Of course I didn't. Thank you." I fired off a quick text. "It's a good thing he was so preoccupied today. He didn't bat an eye when I said Molly and I would be walking to your house." My phone beeped.

Julia handed me the wine and we sat at the kitchen table. "Who's the text from? Is it Derek?"

"I doubt it. He still hasn't called, and last night he didn't even send a text. I think it's safe to say, we aren't getting married on Christmas Eve. How did I get here again?"

"Nia, I'm sorry. Is there anything I can do?"

"Do you have any Julia wisdom? Or do I need to grow a pair and move on?"

"You know me. I don't like to blow smoke up people's asses and tell them what they want to hear."

"No one would ever accuse you of that."

"Right. So, I'm going to give it to you straight. You will be getting married on Christmas Eve."

"As you would say, no offense, but this could be the first time you're actually wrong about something."

"Not a chance. I never told you this, but Phillip freaked out right before the wedding."

"He did? What happened?"

"He just wasn't himself, and instead of leaving him alone to figure it out, I was like a dog with a bone. Finally, he told me it wasn't me he was unsure about, but marriage in general, since he was already divorced twice. We didn't talk for a whole week, but when he called me, he was more committed than ever. He just needed a little time to himself. That's all Derek is doing, taking a little time for him."

"There is a part of me that's glad he's not here. I'm still kind of mad he accused me of leaking Eden's secret. Actually, I'm still mad he went postal on me after my bachelorette party and left with Molly. God, that pissed me off."

"It's not good for you to hang on to that. You can't really move on if you do."

"Fair enough, Dr. Roma."

She laughed. "Have you seen her lately?"

"No. She's been gone since October. She went to Europe. A colleague of hers took over, but you know me, I don't like change, so I quit going. She should be back by now. Maybe I'll call her tomorrow. You know who else I haven't seen. Marshall. It's like he fell off the face of the earth."

"Yeah, you're right."

"The last time I saw him was right after Brooke's engagement party. After that, he had someone else bring the Stargazer lilies to the house. I asked about him, and his delivery guy got really nervous and said he was busy. Since when is Marshall too busy to come over to stare at Derek? They were supposed to deliver more lilies yesterday and no one came. I called the shop this morning and no one answered the phone."

Julia smirked. "Isn't that irritating? When someone doesn't answer their phone. By the way, you haven't read your text message."

I chuckled. "Thanks for being the phone police." I checked it. "It's from Jake. He wants to know where I'll be in an hour. He has a very important errand to run. I'll tell him to pick me up here. I gave Shannon a spare key, so I wouldn't have to run into Walter." I answered his text. "There, Sheriff Julia. I wrote him back."

"Thank you. I thought for sure that text was from Derek."

"Nope. Not hearing from him isn't helping the anger subside, that's for sure."

Julia took a sip of wine and squared her shoulders. "Okay. I'm going to say something, and I want you to listen."

"Oh dear. You have that look you get when you're about to say something profound or that will piss me off. Let me take a drink." I gulped a generous portion of wine. "Okay. Go for it."

"You and Derek are too hard on each other."

"That's it?"

"That's major. Think about it for a second. You never cut each other a break. You don't just get mad you get furious. And it seems like it's not a just a fight it's a blow up and you question the entire relationship."

Julia's words sunk in. She was right, again. I raised a glass. "Thank you. If I ever actually hear from Derek again, I will keep it in mind."

"Here's to that. And to Shannon and Walter."

"I'd never thought I'd toast them, but if it makes Shannon happy, then cheers."

"That was really nice of you to help her out."

"I just hope Walter doesn't break her heart again."

Molly and Sammy trotted in and plunked their heads into the water bowls. After they quenched their thirst, they pranced over to me, resting their chins on my lap.

"Hi, cute pooches. I think they're both worn out." My phone beeped again.

"Maybe it's Derek."

"No. That's weird. It's Vivian. She said Shannon decided to do her own hair and makeup and didn't need her."

Julia scrunched up her face. "That doesn't make any sense."

"I know. She was so excited about it. Let me call Shannon and see what's up."

"Yeah. Call her."

"It went to voicemail. I'll send her a text."

"Maybe we should go to your house, just to make sure she's all right."

"I'll just run down to the house and check on her."

I got up from the table and hurried to the door. Sammy and Molly followed.

"Do you want me to come with you?"

"No. Enjoy your wine. I just remembered, Vivian has purple hair now. Maybe that freaked Shannon out.

I'm sure it's nothing."

Sammy and Molly had hopeful wagging tails when I got to the door. "Hey, Julia, will you call them. They want to come with me."

"Okay. Sammy, Molly, does anyone want a treat. Come get a treat." That did the trick.

Boy, it sure got dark early these days. I reached into the pocket of my jacket to see if Shannon texted back. *Ah shit!* I left my phone at Julia's house. I would've headed back to get it, but I saw a cab pull up in front of Walter's house. Only it wasn't Walter getting out of the cab.

A woman with a slight build climbed out. The driver retrieved her bags. She tipped him, shook her head no, and waved him off.

"Hi," I called to her.

She turned and I caught a glimpse of her face under the street light. It was worn and pale. The dark brown hair pulled into a bun on top of her head bore streaks of noticeable grey. "Hello," she said with soft voice. "Can I help you?"

"Actually, I was going to ask if I could help you with your bags. I was on my way home."

Bolstered with determination, she gripped the handles of her suitcases. "Thank you. But as I explained to the driver, I can manage." She lifted with all her might and barely budged them off the ground. "Perhaps I'm a little tired from the flight."

"No worries. I got them." I picked them up and we

trudged up the walkway to Walter's front door. Who was this woman visiting Walter on the night he was supposed to propose?

"Thank you. That's very kind. It's been a long day."

"My pleasure. So, are you visiting?"

"No. I live here."

"You live here? In this house? Did you just buy it?"

"No. I'm sorry, I didn't get your name."

I set the bags down on the porch. "Oh, I'm Nia. I live down the street."

She offered her hand. "I'm Dorothy. Dorothy Wall."

All the air left my lungs, and my hand trembled in hers. "You're Larry Wall's wife?"

"Ex-wife, actually. Nice to meet you, Nia... Nia? Are you Nia Kelly?"

I exhaled. "Yes."

"My poor dear. What you've endured because of my ex-husband. You're visibly shaken. Would you like to come in the house and get a drink of water or something?"

"No... No, you don't understand. Until recently, someone has been living in your house. Did you rent it to a man named Walter? Walter James?"

"No. I don't know anyone by that name. Did you say his last name was James?"

"Yes. He's tall, early forties. Do you know him?"

"Leave the bags, and come inside for a minute. I hope I'm wrong about this."

We walked inside and the house definitely had a refined women's touch. Dorothy rushed to the closet. "These pictures are old, but I want you to take a look." She rifled through a photo album. "Is this the man who's been living here?"

A young Walter James stared back at me in the picture. "Yes. That's him. That's Walter."

"That's not his name. His name is James. That's Larry's brother. James Wall."

Panic and fear gripped every cell of my body. "Oh God, Shannon. Oh no. I've got to go."

"What it is it?"

"I can't explain, but Larry's brother has been living in your house. He's in town. Be careful. Don't open the door." I fled to the porch.

"Nia. Wait. Should I call the police?"

"I don't know. I've got to get to my friend."

I ran like the wind to my house. It was pitch-black. *Fuck!* Why didn't I have my phone? I should've told Dorothy to call the police. Shannon could be in trouble.

I didn't use my key. I scaled the side gate and shimmied through the doggie door. I couldn't tell if anyone was here. I tiptoed up the stairs. There was a hint of light coming from Derek's office and our bedroom. My heart pounded so loud, I thought my chest would split open. With one cautious step at a time, I made my way to the bedroom.

Shit! Shannon was in my bathrobe, bound and gagged, face down on my bed. My jewelry was strewn about next to her.

I placed my hand on her shoulder and she jerked. "Shh... It's okay. I'm going to get us out of here."

I eased her upright and removed the gag. Her eyes filled with terror. "I'm so scared."

I whispered, "I'm scared too."

"Is Derek back in town?"

"No. I wished to God he was. I'm sorry. But we can get through this."

Her voice was faint and shaken. "Nia, I'm the one who's sorry. Everything Walter said was a lie."

"I know. His name isn't Walter, it's James Wall. He's Larry's brother. And if Larry is behind this, we have to get the hell out of here."

"Larry's brother!"

"Shh... I saw a light on in Derek's office. Is he in there?"

"Yes. He said he was going to turn the place upside down looking for another safe."

"Okay. That's a good thing. If he wants money and my jewelry, maybe he doesn't want to hurt us. Here, let me untie you. If I can find the key to the patio doors, we can escape." I released her wrists and ankles. "We opened up the doors on Thanksgiving. I don't know what Derek did with the key. Quick, put your jeans and sweater back on. I'll try to find it."

Shannon threw on her clothes lying by the bed. I

rummaged through Derek's nightstand and found the key. "I got it. Let's go."

I grabbed her hand and she froze in place. "Shannon come on."

"Leaving so soon?"

I turned and Larry's brother, James Wall stood before me with menacing eyes that racked me with sheer horror. I held onto Shannon's hand and swallowed hard. "Yes. We're leaving. You've got what you came for. Take anything you want. Just let us go and we won't call the police. I know who you really are, James."

"Oh. You found me out. Well, Meagan Ryan, I guess you're not the only one who can change their name and pretend to be someone else."

"Did Larry put you up to this?"

"Well, I suppose he would have a little ax to grind now, wouldn't he? You sent my brother to jail. You ruined his life."

"Your brother, Larry sent himself to jail. If you don't want to end up there yourself, I suggest you let us go."

He folded his arms and took threatening steps toward us. Shannon began to cry. I put my arm around her. "Look, Shannon has nothing to do with this. How about we let her go?"

James smiled. "How about, I don't fucking think so. Get on your knees. Both of you."

We sank to the floor, trembling and clutching one

another. "Good." James wrapped my hair around his hand and pulled. "My brother said you were a sweet little piece of ass, and such a fucking tease. He was right. Now, this is what's going to happen. You're going to suck my dick. Get it nice and wet, and then I'm going to shove it in your ass. I bet it's a tight virgin asshole too. Once I'm finished with you, Shannon, sweetheart, you get sloppy seconds."

Shannon and I convulsed in a sea of tears. I closed my eyes and prayed. I didn't want this man's hands on me for a moment, let alone take something that belonged to Derek. *Oh God, Derek. I love you. Wherever you are, I love you.*

James unzipped his pants and taunted me.

Shannon released her grip from my shoulders, and I coiled my arms around myself, sobbing uncontrollably.

"I can't wait to feel those beautiful lips around my cock. I got hard just thinking about it."

I heard a click. "Get the fuck away from her," Shannon screamed.

Jesus fuck! She had gun! Where the fuck did she get a gun?

James backed up in a frenzy toward the loveseat. "Shannon, put the gun down. I didn't mean what I said. I wasn't going to touch to her, I swear."

"It didn't look that way to me. Is that what you wanted this whole time? To fuck her in the ass?"

"No. You've got to believe me. I wouldn't have done it. I took things too far. I'm sorry, put down the gun."

I spotted Shannon's phone peeking out of the pocket of my bathrobe. While she held James at gunpoint, I turned and grabbed it to call the police.

Cold metal pressed into the back of my head. "Drop it, Nia. You're not calling anybody."

I dropped the phone and glanced up. Shannon held the gun to my head. "Shannon, what are you doing? You're my friend."

Her eyes glazed over and her demeanor changed. She was morphing into someone else before my eyes. "I was never your friend. But I fooled you, didn't I? Either I'm an incredible actress, or you're a fucking idiot. Get up." She yanked me up by my jacket and pushed me toward the wall by the door, keeping the gun on me. "Okay, James. Get the jewelry."

I shook like a leaf with my hands up. "Shannon, how could you? I trusted you."

"You want to know the truth? At first, I didn't want any part of this. But then, I found you so damn annoying. The way you constantly threw yourself at James disgusted me."

"But I never—"

"Shut up! You almost convinced him to walk away from Larry's plan, but then I told him about the new necklace Derek bought you—an easy hundred grand."

James collected the jewelry on the bed, shoving it into our pillowcases. "I'm sorry, Nia, but the ten grand Derek gave me to leave town didn't cut it. We've been swimming in debt because of Larry's legal bills." He reached for my mom's wedding ring.

"Please don't take my mom's ring. It's all I have left of her. Her ring and her jewelry box. Please."

"Oh spare me!" Shannon chided. She picked up my mother's jewelry box and hurled it at me. It hit the wall and smashed to bits.

I fell to the ground, clutching the cherry wood pieces. "Why! Why are you doing this? Why do you hate me so much?"

"Because I had a pretty decent life in California with James, until Larry showed up penniless to live on our couch. That was your fault. It's been one long shit show after that. Our lives consumed with his revenge, even when he was in prison. Oh, and let's not forget you think the world revolves around you and your little crisis of the moment. God, you're such a fucking whiner. Poor Nia with her rich fiancé and jewelry she doesn't even want. You make me sick."

She took two steps toward me and James stopped her. "Shannon, that's enough. Put the gun down. We got what we came for. Let's go." He came to me and helped me to my feet. "Here's your mom's ring. I'm sorry I scared you before. I swear I wasn't going to hurt you. Shannon said you texted her and were probably on your way. I got carried away with the charade. It was all an act to throw you off."

When I peered into his eyes, I saw kindness and sincerity. "It's okay," I whispered. "Don't let her kill me. Please don't let her kill me." As a sign of assurance, he slid my mom's wedding ring on my finger.

"Jesus," Shannon yelled. "What a fucking whore. You're doing it again. Throwing yourself at my man." She fired a bullet into the jewelry armoire Derek got me, and the sudden realization that I may never see him again strangled me in agony. Then Shannon aimed the gun on me. "You must have a death wish."

"I don't. Please, you have to believe me. I love Derek. He's the love of my life, and I want more than anything to marry him. And I know James loves you. You can still walk away from this and have a future together. Just drop the gun. If our friendship ever met anything to you, even for a second, please let me go."

"Nia's right. Sweetheart, we'll take the jewelry and ride off into the sunset, just like we talked about for months."

"Listen to him, Shannon. He's offering you the future you've always wanted. Just let me walk out of here. I won't call the police. I swear it."

The look on her face was beyond insane. She laughed low in her throat. "You must think James is some kind of knight in shining armor. You would be wrong. The only reason he doesn't want me to shoot you is because he made a promise, to his big brother Larry to let him do it. I guess you could say, Larry is dying to kill you. And he's coming for you."

My eyes met with James'. He shook his head. "In

the end, I tried to help you. I really did. You don't deserve this." He placed his hands on my shoulder. "I'm sorry."

"Don't touch her!" Shannon shrieked.

James backed off. "Fine!"

"I just thought of something. I didn't promise Larry anything." She cocked the gun.

"Shannon, no! Stop!" James dove in front of me.

The gun went off and I screamed. "Oh my God! No! James! You shot him!"

Shannon dropped the gun and collapsed to the floor in wailing sobs. "No! No! I didn't mean it! Please God. I didn't mean it."

His lifeless body reposed on the carpet with blood spurting from his chest. He took a bullet for me and there was nothing I could do for him. Now that I knew what Shannon was capable of, I scrambled to grab her phone and ran down the stairs. Her bellows of agony grew louder when I reached the front door. I frantically flipped on the lights and dialed 911. "Come on, pick up." I opened the door and came face-to-face with my unthinkable nightmare.

I dropped the phone and heaved. "Larry."

His terrifying glare was like a laser of evil. "Well, finally, Nia Kelly, we meet again. I've been waiting for this moment for a long time. I wouldn't rush off if I were you."

The tips of his fingers pressed on my chest, pushing me backward toward the stairs. My trembling jelly legs could barely hold me upright. He shut the front door. Everything happened so fast, my head spun in a whirlpool of terror.

Larry heard Shannon's cries. His eyes darted to the top of the stairs. "What's going on?" I was so frightened I couldn't speak. What's he going to do to me after he finds out his brother is dead? He cracked me hard across the face. "Tell me. Now!"

"Shannon pulled a gun on me. I…got it away from her…and…and…I hit her. That's it."

"Where's my brother?"

The back of my calf met with the first step. I inched my way to the left, so I wouldn't end up defenseless, pinned against the stairs. Larry countered my movement. "I'll ask again. Where is my brother?"

"He left. He said he didn't want any part of this and took off."

Larry brought his face close to mine. The stench of his nasty breath turned my stomach. "I knew he'd go soft when it came to you. Not me. I'm hard as a rock. I'm going to fuck you and then kill you, Nia Kelly. And I'm going to enjoy every second of it. I learned a few things in prison. This is going to be like my homecoming."

A loud cry sounded from the bedroom. "James! He's so cold. Oh God!"

Larry dashed halfway up the stairs. "Shannon! What's going on?"

"James is dead. It's Nia's fault. I didn't mean it. I

swear to God, it was an accident."

This was it. If he rushed to his brother's side, I could make a run for it. I cowered around the stairs and bumped into the table with the flowers. The vase. My left hand reached behind my back and I clutched it tight.

Larry's eyes flashed in a crazy rage as he flew down the stairs. "You killed my brother?"

My body quaked in despair. "No. Shannon shot him. I'm telling you the truth."

He grasped me by the throat. "She said it was your fault. How come when anything bad happens in my life, you're right there. You're to blame for all of this." He squeezed on my windpipe. "I can't wait to watch my bare hands drain the life out of your body."

A vision of Derek's beautiful face swept through my brain. I was going to die, and Derek would never know how much I truly loved him. I squeaked out, "Just do it. Kill me. As long as you're alive, my life will be hell." He lightened his grip with a quizzical expression. Telling him to kill me threw Larry off guard. Somewhere deep within I felt him. I felt my connection to Derek. I had to fight.

"Come on, Larry. What are you waiting for? Kill me."

He released my throat and my left hand swung the vase, bashing him in the side of the head. He cried out in pain, went down with a thud, and blood streamed from his head. He wasn't moving. Oh God, did I kill him?

Shannon appeared at the top of the staircase, gun in hand. "Oh my God, Larry. What've you done? You're going to pay for this!"

I sped out the door screaming at the top of my lungs. "Help me! Please! Somebody! Help!"

I spotted someone at the edge of the walkway. It was so dark I couldn't see who it was, but I ran to them. "Please help me. Do you have a phone? Call 911! Oh Jesus. Fuck! Stay away from me."

"I already called the police. You're going to have to trust me, Nia. I'm the only friend you got."

"Sonya. What are you doing here?"

"Trying to save your ass. I'm on your side."

"Then we need to get out of here. James is dead, and I think I killed Larry. Shannon has a gun. She's lost her mind."

Molly and Sammy came barreling toward me. "Oh shit. No, Molly. Sammy no. Sonya, let's go. Come on."

Sonya gasped. "Oh no!"

Shannon, drunk with insanity and wielding her gun, bounded off the porch. "I hate you, Nia!"

Sammy growled and I captured their collars. "Stay with me." Both wriggled. "No, no. Please stay."

Shannon slowly closed in on us. "You took James away from me. You're the one who should be dead."

"Sonya, did you really call the police?"

"Yes. Now get behind me."

"What are you talking about? What are you

doing?"

"Something I should've done a long time ago, protect you. Get behind me."

"I can't let you do that."

She stood in front of me. "I have to."

In the distance, I saw headlights headed in our direction like a beacon in the night.

Shannon fired a warning shot into the air. Molly and Sammy went berserk. There was no calming them down. "The next bullet is for you, Nia. You fucking bitch."

Sonya shouted, "Shannon, drop the gun. I've called the police. You're only making it worse for yourself."

"Sonya! You're a goddamn traitor. I knew it. I knew we shouldn't have trusted you. Have it your way. I don't care if the bullet goes through you, as long as it hits Nia."

She fired off another bullet into the ground and laugh maniacally. "Scared you, didn't I?"

Sammy and Molly barked, and squirmed. "Sammy, sit. Molly, stop. Molly, please."

Shannon leveled the gun at us. "Come here, Molly. Molly, come."

Molly broke free and fled to Shannon. "Molly, no!" I ran after her, and threw my body on top of hers. I heard the screeching of a car and Sonya scream.

The gun went off and a searing pain burned through me. There was so much noise, like an explosion. The shrieks and cries. Derek, where are you?

Everything we fought about was so meaningless... I love you. That's all that matters. Oh God, Derek, please. Please be here. Don't let her take me away from you. I squinted and I thought I saw...is it really you? Derek, it hurts. *Oh my God...no... I can't... I love you, Derek, so much...but it hurts... I'm sorry.*

My world faded to black.

Chapter Fourteen

A faint constant beep registered in my brain. My mouth was dry, and my eyes felt like they were glued shut with a thick layer of paste. *Where am I? How long have I been here? God, if this is heaven, I'm not impressed.*

My head pounded and my left ass cheek stung with a biting pain. All I wanted was Derek. I concentrated and focused my energies. "De–De–Derek?" Fingertips brushed over my forehead. "De–Derek–Derek?"

"Shhh… Don't try to talk, angel. Just rest. I'm right here."

I had to see him, feel him, tell him I loved him. It took all my strength to pry open my eyes and find his gorgeous blue eyes looking into mine.

"There's my beautiful girl." He kissed my forehead. "Nurse. She's awake."

"That's good news, Mr. Pierce. Let me get Doctor Parker."

I reached for his hand. "So, I'm not dead?"

He smiled, sat on the bed, and took my hand. "No. You're going to be just fine. And Molly's fine, and so is Sammy."

"Did Shannon shoot me?"

"Yes, but it's not serious. The bullet only grazed

you. You were lucky. It could've been worse."

Derek's hand in mine was definitely the healing touch I needed. He was here. I felt our powerful connection surge, and the fog in my head began to dissipate. "I was all wrong about Sonya. She tried to help me. I remember. She told me to stand behind her."

I rubbed my eyes. "How long have I been out? I don't remember anything after I dove on top of Molly."

"Not that long. You hit your head pretty hard when you saved Molly. You have a mild concussion."

Flashes of the terrifying night came flooding back. "Derek, I was so scared... I–I thought I was going to die...and...I would never get to...tell you..."

"Hi. I'm Doctor Parker. How's the patient doing?"

Derek shook the middle-aged, balding Doctor's hand. "I'm predicting she'll be back to her feisty self in no time, Doctor Parker."

"Please call me Lou. My wife Tracey is such a fan. She will faint when I tell her I met you. I wish it was under better circumstances for Nia's sake. Let's have a look." He shined a light in my eyes and I tracked his finger back and forth. "Good." He glanced at my chart. "Your vitals are on track as well. I just need to check your wound."

"If it looks good, can I go home now?"

He came around the left side of the bed. "Just as a precaution, we'd like to keep you here for the night. That's why your husband requested the best room and an extra large bed, so he could stay with you."

"My husband? How hard did I hit my head?"

Derek whispered in my ear, "Just go with it."

"Could you roll on your side for me, Nia?" Doctor Parker asked. He peeled back the bandage. "Okay. Looks good. This will heal in no time. You were very lucky."

"It didn't feel lucky. It hurts like a son of a bitch."

Doctor Parker laughed. "Well, it seems like your pain meds have kicked in nicely."

"Actually, Lou," Derek said. "That's just, Nia. One might say she has a very dirty little mouth. I wouldn't have her any other way." He pressed his lips to mine.

"I can't wait to go home and tell my wife Tracey that Derek Pierce and his new bride got their happily ever after. You'll be released tomorrow, Nia. Just finish your antibiotics and rest for a few days."

Derek and the doctor shook hands again. "Thank you, Lou. I'll take good care of her."

"I'm sure you will. The world could use more heroes like you," Doctor Parker said before leaving my room.

"Hero?" I asked, "What was Doctor Parker talking about... Derek...were you...there? I thought...I just imagined it. Where you really there?"

Derek sat on the bed. "Yes, sweetie, I was there. Shannon was going to shoot you again and I..."

My eyes welled up with tears. "You saved me. You saved my life." I opened my arms to him and he swept me away with his embrace.

"I wish I would've gotten there sooner. I should've been there."

I sobbed. "I thought I was going to die. You saved me."

"Shh… It's okay. Don't cry. You're safe. Hey, I had a little help from your buddy Sammy."

"You did?"

"Yeah. After I wrestled Shannon to the ground and got the gun, Sammy pounced on her and held her in place until the police put her in handcuffs."

I wiped my tears. "Good old Sammy. He's always had my back. Can I ask you something else? While I was conked out, did you marry me or something? The Doctor called you my husband."

He brought my hand to his mouth and kissed it. "If I would've thought of it, I would have. But, in this instance, it was the only way I could stay with you. Only family is allowed to spend the night. And you're my family. There was no way I was leaving."

"Really? But, I'm still so confused. You haven't called. You didn't even text me last night." I adjusted the bandage on my butt. "Ow! Fuck that hurts!"

"Here, sweetie. Press that button on your IV. It's for the pain."

"Thank you."

"You'll feel so much better tomorrow when you get out of here. Hey, what is it, baby?"

"I just don't understand. How are you even here? I thought you changed your mind and you didn't want to marry me anymore."

"Come here." He swaddled me back into his arms and I broke down again. "Oh, my angel. Nothing could be further from the truth. In fact, I was already on my way here. Remember when Jake said he had an errand to run? He was on his way to pick me up."

"But I haven't heard from you."

He gently rocked me and calmed me down. "I know. And we're going to talk about everything, but not now. Put it out of your mind and sleep. You've been through hell."

"And you won't leave?"

"I'm not going anywhere."

I peeked up at him. "I mean. You won't leave, ever."

He caressed my face. "I won't leave, ever. I almost lost you tonight. If anything, I love you even more."

"Derek... Tonight...when...Larry... He...he... almost..."

"Please, angel. Don't give him another thought. Let's get you settled. Is the pain medicine working?"

"Yes. I'm really sleepy, but I'm afraid to fall asleep. I'm afraid I'll have a nightmare."

"Then I will hold you that much tighter. Come on. Let's get you tucked in."

Before he said his usual "Goodnight, my sweet girl, I love you" I was asleep.

* * * *

"I killed him! Oh God! I killed him!"

"Baby, wake up! It's just a dream."

Derek flipped on the light. My eyes searched for his. "Did I kill him? Is Larry dead? Am I going to jail? Derek, I'm scared. I'm so scared."

His strong arms clutched me to his chest. "Don't be scared. I'm right here."

"But what happened? Where is he? Did Larry go back to jail?"

"Don't give that scumbag another thought. I wish you had killed him."

I broke our embrace. "Derek, you know something. Where is he?"

He exhaled. "He's here."

"What? That's crazy."

"I know. The ambulance brought both of you here. It's fucked-up. He's in a different wing and there are guards at his door, but he shouldn't be here. There's a policeman outside your door too."

"So, I didn't kill him?"

"No. But, he'll be going to jail for the rest of his life. And so is Shannon."

"Walter took a bullet for me. I mean, James. Walter was really James Wall, Larry's brother. Oh God, our house. There's so much blood."

"Jake is taking care of the house. He called a service of some kind. By the time we get home, tomorrow, it'll be fine, but if you don't want to live there anymore, we'll move. Whatever you want. I'll buy Steve and Scott's house, if you want."

"Well, that would be great. It's right next to Julia's, plus, I mean, come on, they're gay. They have way better taste than you do. Have you seen their fixtures?"

Derek smiled. "Now there's my girl. Consider it done. You never have to set foot in the house again, if you don't want to."

"I don't. Maybe we can stay with Julia until we get everything moved."

"Sure. That sounds like a plan. Do you think you could go back to sleep for me?"

"I could. But there's just one problem. I have to go to the bathroom."

"Okay. I'll take you."

"I can go by myself, or we could call the nurse."

"I'm not letting you out of my sight for a second. I'm taking you."

I wheeled the IV on my left and Derek came to my right side. "Lean on me, sweetie. We'll go nice and slow."

I put one foot in front of the other and took baby steps to the bathroom. My legs grew more solid with each small stride.

"That's my good girl. Do you need help sitting on the toilet?"

"No. But could you hold the IV steady?"

"Of course. Ease yourself down. There you go. Are you in pain?"

"No. The bullet hit me on the side of my cheek, I can sit."

He got on his knees, eye level with me. "I'm grateful there won't be any permanent damage to your perfect little ass. You know, I'm quite fond of that area."

I smiled. "You might say rather obsessed. Um... Do you think you could close your eyes? I can't pee if you're looking at me."

He placed his hand on my knee. "Of course, my sweet girl."

Derek closed his eyes. There should've been a huge ick factor in this moment, but it was the ultimate in taking care of me. It was in sickness and in health, real life dedication. It was what a husband would do for his wife.

When I was finished, he reached for the toilet paper. "Derek, I can do it."

"Baby, you're left-handed and you're hooked up to the IV. How many times have I gotten you a warm washcloth to tend to you? This isn't any different. Let me help you." I nodded and he dried me off. "There. All done. Was that so bad?"

"No," I said quietly.

Derek washed his hands and then kissed my forehead. "Come on. Let's get you back to bed. Put your right arm around my neck." He hoisted me up and tucked into my side.

"I'd kill for a shower right now."

"We'll have to ask them in the morning if I can put you in the tub. If not, I give a killer sponge bath."

I toddled along more sure-footed. "That sounds like heaven. It kind of turned me on. Do you want to have sex?"

Derek laughed. "Not tonight. You have a headache."

I giggled. "Good point. Can we watch TV?"

"No, sweetie. Right to sleep."

"You're awfully bossy, Mr. Pierce."

"I am, Miss Kelly. Bossy and madly in love with you."

* * * *

The next morning, I woke up in Derek's arms with less pain and even more love for him. It wasn't long before my room filled with flowers and my gang.

Julia and Phillip convinced the hospital that Molly was my therapy dog. They were in my room along with Jake and Lacey, sporting a blender. It was protein smoothies for everyone, the breakfast of champions. I was due to be released in the afternoon. Until then, it was party time, hospital style.

"Oh look, Nia, the Stargazer lilies are from Marshall," Julia said. "I talked to him this morning. He was in Minnesota. His dad passed away. That's why we haven't heard from him."

"I'm so sorry to hear that. I should be the one

sending him flowers."

"He won't be in town long enough. He's headed back to Minnesota to take care of his dad's house and estate."

"I hope he's okay."

"He sounded good. He's worried about you."

"Just like the rest of us." Lacey sat on the edge of the bed. "How are you feeling?"

"I'm fine, physically. Just still coming to terms with Walter, I mean, James taking a bullet for me, and Shannon, she fooled us all."

"She did. I can't imagine how awful last night was for you."

"All of you being here, is the best medicine. Isn't that right, Molly?" She gave kisses. "See, all better."

"I'm sorry to interrupt." Sonya stood at the doorway.

"Sonya," I exclaimed. "Please come in."

"I was wondering if it would be okay if we talked in private?" she asked.

"Yes, of course. You guys don't mind?"

"No. We should get going and let Nia rest," Phillip responded.

"Your room will be ready," Julia added. "You guys can stay with us as long as you like."

Lacey hugged me. "I better get back to the club. Someone's got to run that joint."

"Thank you. Thank you all for coming."

Jake came to the bed and draped his arm over

Lacey. "Feel better, Nia."

Derek kissed my forehead. "I'm going to let you talk to Sonya. I want to find out what's going on with Larry Wall." He shook Sonya's hand. "Thank you. Thank you for what you did for Nia. I won't forget it."

Everyone filed out the door, except for Nurse Molly, who cuddled next to me, lapping up remnants of my smoothie.

Sonya sat in the chair next to the bed. There was not a hint of a scowl. This was a woman who'd been to hell and back. She was a survivor.

"Sonya, I don't know what to say. Thank you. I should've listened to Brooke. You really did want to help me."

"It was risky for me to even approach Brooke. But it was the least I could do, after I helped Larry and Nick. Your life has been in danger ever since I told Larry the information on your application. I had no right, and started something in motion that I couldn't stop."

"I have to ask. Why did you dislike me so much? What did I do wrong?"

"You did nothing wrong. It was me. I had worked for the club for over ten years, and not once had anyone invited me to the club for so much as a drink. Now, I know we weren't supposed to socialize. But you showed up and had the world at your feet. You were best friends with Julia and Brooke. The members raved about what a great teacher you were, and the only man who'd shown me the slightest bit of attention in years, suddenly had his eye on you. It just ate away at me. Then a celebrity shows up, and who does he fall for? You. I'm ashamed, Nia. But jealousy is such a powerful thing. It drove me to do unspeakable things."

"I'm sorry you felt that way. I never meant to—"

"I know. None of this is your fault. When Larry painted you as a slutty runaway wife, I was so bitter toward you, I wanted to believe it. After you were nearly killed by Nick, and I realized I was wrong about you, I had to make it right. That's why I pretended to be in on Larry's scheme. It was the only way I could help you."

"So, everything that happened, Brooke had nothing to do with it?"

"No. She was your true friend. Larry was the master manipulator. He even convinced Nick's parents to file the lawsuit against Metro. Then turned over the correspondence with Nick to make himself look like the good guy. Shannon and James, they led Melissa to you and told her you had a puppy, but Larry was the ringleader."

"That day Melissa showed up at the house. She tried to tell me something and Nick's parents stopped her."

"She probably wanted to warn you about Shannon. In the beginning, she went along with it, so she could hang onto her relationship with James. But as you could probably tell, James fell for you and it made Shannon crazy. She was not the most stable person to begin with. Did you notice her mood swings?"

"Now that you mention it, yes. It seemed like Walter, sorry James, dictated her mood."

"I think you're right about that. Well, despite everything, I just hope someday, you'll be able to forgive me."

I reached for her hand. "Sonya, I already have. You need to forgive yourself."

She clasped my hand and hung her head. "Thank you. I'll try."

Derek hurried into the room visibly shaken. "Sonya. Good. You're still here."

"Derek, what is it?" I asked.

He exhaled. "It's Larry Wall. Early this morning he committed suicide. He's dead."

I gasped. "Oh my God!" Sonya put her head in her hands. "Sonya, are you okay?"

She gave a faint nod. "Yes. I'm actually relieved, for your sake and mine. He would never have stopped." She rose from her chair. "I'm going to get going. You take care of yourself and each other. Marry this man and have beautiful babies. I will be cheering and praying for you in my own way. God bless you."

"You too, Sonya. Take care."

She left and Derek sat on the bed and drew me into his arms. "It's over, Nia. It's finally over. There are no more threats, and nothing to fear."

"Is it terrible that I feel relieved too?"

"No. I agree with Sonya. He would've never stopped." Derek released me from his embrace and smoothed the hair off my face. "I agree with Sonya about something else. You should marry me and have our beautiful babies."

My eyes filled with tears. "Derek, there's something I've been trying to tell you. I need to say it."

"Of course, sweetie."

"When Larry had his hand gripped around my throat, I really thought he was going to kill me. And in that moment, all I could think about was you. I was afraid I was going to die and you would never know how much I truly love you, because I do. I really love you. I love you. I love you so much."

I broke down in sobs and he cradled me in his arms. "I love you too. Shhh…baby. Don't cry. Nia, does this mean you'll still marry me on Christmas Eve?"

I peered into his beautiful blue eyes. "Yes. Let's get married. I want to be your wife. I want to be yours."

Chapter Fifteen

The next few weeks were a whirlwind of activity. We moved into Steve and Scott's house and partook in heavy-duty therapy sessions with Doctor Roma. Turns out, when Derek was in LA, he was already on the phone with her an hour a day, sorting out his issues. He discovered the ending of *First Bite* affected him on a much deeper level than he realized. After all, the show changed his life and made him a huge star. Also, as much as he wanted to be in charge on his new show, *The Alec Stone Chronicles*, the looming responsibility of producing and starring began to wear on him. The entire time he was in LA after the fight, one thing never wavered, how much he longed to marry me. He just needed a little time to himself. Julia was right, again

The nightmares subsided shortly after we moved into our new house. Derek was more relaxed and attentive than ever. While we no longer needed Jake as a bodyguard, Derek kept him on as our driver, except when we were in LA.

Jake and Lacey took their trip to Hawaii for Christmas. Since our wedding was on-again, off-again, I didn't mind they would miss our ceremony. I gave them my blessing in hopes Lacey might come back engaged.

The fitness room was finally being expanded, and classes ceased the second week of December. A Las Vegas Casino mogul, Adam Maxwell, bought the country club. I heard he was changing the name to The Vegas Edge and giving it a major overhaul. Sue Peterson told me she saw him at the BDSM club, and according to Sue, he was a dark Adonis and a Dominant. I wasn't exactly sure what that meant, so she explained it to me. After I thought about it, in some ways, in the bedroom, I suppose, Derek was dominant as well. We just never put a label on it. Now it made me curious to go to that secret club.

The one regret I had as the wedding drew near was Brooke. I missed her so much. There were times I picked up the phone to call her, but was worried she would never be able to forgive me. While the Larry Wall incident didn't make national news, I wondered if she heard about it. Although as each day came and went, I realized I might never see her again.

It was December 23. I was in Derek's living room in LA. The decorations for our wedding tomorrow night were impeccable. Two grand Christmas trees flagged the mantle with white lights and assorted gold, red, and green shiny ornaments. The manger scene, sitting atop the mantle was exquisite and charming. The fire crackled and glowed. Yes, this room was like Derek, perfection.

He was going to get the shock of his life when he came home from happy hour with his dad, Keith, and

Tim. It was Derek's version of a bachelor party. It was sweet and much tamer than mine.

Molly and I were supposed to spend the night at Derek's parents' house. At the last minute, I changed the plan. Actually, I obliterated it. I was sleeping here and Molly was having a slumber party at her grandparents' house.

I spent the day with Valerie, shopping for my wedding dress. If my own mother couldn't be with me, I was touched Derek's mom volunteered to step in. It took no time at all. I had a general idea of what I wanted. It was the first dress I tried on, strapless, formfitting, and simple. The champagne color warmed my skin tone, and the thick satin ribbon around the waist gave a little something special. I couldn't wait to walk down the staircase tomorrow night and marry Derek in this room.

After I got home from shopping, I took another shower to wipe away the LA grime. I grabbed up the comforters in the guest bedrooms and spread them across the floor. David, Derek's housekeeper, shot me a quizzical expression and I promptly sent him on his way.

Then I scampered back upstairs to don my holiday sex outfit, red bustie', with panties, garters, stockings, and high heels. I covered it up with a Santa inspired robe. Before I left the bedroom, I placed Derek's surprise into my pocket.

When he walked into the living room, he would

find me in my Christmas ensemble, the blankets, a glass of Jordan Cabernet, mistletoe, and something else he wasn't expecting.

I heard a click of the door and stood to primp myself while my heart sped up. With mistletoe in hand, I glanced over at the manger scene and thought about what was going to happen next. It was so going to make the baby Jesus cry.

Derek's footsteps made their way to the staircase. I called to him, "Santa's made an early delivery."

He turned and his face lit up with delight. "What…? What are you doing here? I thought you and Molly were spending the night at my parents."

I held the mistletoe over my head. "Well, guess what? I changed the plan!"

He wasted zero time sweeping me up into a spellbinding kiss. His lips were tinged with a hint of wine. As always he was delicious."

"You look so cute in your Santa suit. And the mistletoe is an excellent touch."

I tossed it on the floor. "Well, I was going to fasten it to my thong, but I was afraid I'd have a mistletoe camel toe situation."

He threw his head back and laughed. "Come here." He sealed our bodies together and rested his forehead on mine. "I'm so glad you changed the plan."

I reached into my pocket. "Derek, I didn't just change it. I bitch-slapped it." I showed him the bottle of lube. His eyes grew wild with excitement when I placed the bottle in his hand. "Christmas is coming early, Mr. Pierce. And so are we."

He smiled and cupped my face. "Baby, are you sure? You said you wanted to wait until we're married."

"But, in so many ways, I already feel like your wife. I vow right now to honor and cherish you all the days of my life."

"I noticed you left out obey."

"In the bedroom, when we're playing, I vow to obey."

He arched his eyebrow. "Really?"

"Well, I vow to *obey-ish*."

"That's what I thought. But are you absolutely sure you want to do this right now?"

"Yes. When I walk down those stairs tomorrow night, I want to know that every part of me is already yours, fully and completely."

"I want that too. Tomorrow will be kind of crazy with everyone coming in."

"What do you mean? It's just Julia, Phillip, and the dogs?"

"I just mean in some ways the wedding could take over. And I won't even get to see you until tomorrow night when you come down the aisle. So, this is perfect. Tonight is just for us."

"We'll be in the bubble."

He grinned. "Yes, the bubble."

"Do you want some wine? I poured us a glass of Cabernet."

He spotted the wine on the hearth of the fireplace. "Yes. I see you gave us each a 'Nia pour.'"

"What's a 'Nia pour?'"

"You know, half the bottle in each glass."

I pressed my lips to his. "Well, you know me, Mr. Pierce. I don't like to fuck around."

"Hmmm...I do, Miss Kelly. I like to fuck around with you. But tonight, I want to take my time with you. I want it to be special, for both of us. Come." He motioned for me to get down on the floor with him, handed me a glass and proposed a toast. "To us, baby. To our marriage and the adventure that lies ahead. I'm the luckiest man in the world to have you by my side. So, here's to you, my wife, my Nia. You're the girl of my dreams."

We clinked glasses, exchanged a sweet kiss, and sipped our wine. I soaked the moment in, while I reveled in the aesthetic charm of him. The way his fingers curved around the stem of his wineglass and his stunning hands; his broad shoulders and strong arms—arms that were equally gentle and loving.

Derek took the wineglasses and sat them down. "What is it, sweetie?"

"It's you. Sometimes I still can't believe I'm the girl of your dreams. Especially when...when you're the man of mine. You've made all my dreams come true."

Without one word, he engulfed me in those strong, gentle, loving arms, and consumed me with a kiss that touched my soul. His lips made a sizzling path to my neck. Needy moans and murmurs filled the air. My stomach dizzied as he feasted on me. His mouth reclaimed mine and he crushed me to him. His lips were warm, yet demanding, causing my pussy to spasm as dewy moisture leaked onto my panties.

When he broke our kiss, he had the look, my look; the flaring nostrils; the penetrating eyes—the look I craved. His inviting voice dripped in lust. "Take off your robe, but do it slowly."

My skin flushed under his command. On my knees, I undid the robe and revealed a hint of what was waiting for him underneath. He nodded his head in approval while a devious smile played on his lips. I slipped the robe off my shoulders and gradually let it fall to the ground.

His seductive glare bore into me as his eyes roved over my red bustie', with stockings and garters. He blew out a breath. "Fuck. You're gorgeous. You're like my very own Christmas package that I get to unwrap."

He brushed his fingers along my collarbone and dipped them between my breasts. He continued down my stomach and stopped at my panties. "Mmm…that's a very interesting choice you made, wearing panties, young lady. I wonder if they're wet." He slipped inside examining my saturated state.

I whimpered, "Oh, Derek."

His husky voice whispered, "What do you want me to do, Nia?"

"Tear them off."

"Good girl." He ripped them off my body, and his hand flew back to my aching clit, skating over my slippery folds. "Feel how ready you are for me. God, I can't get enough of it." He popped a finger inside and his other hand tugged on the bustie'. "Take this off."

I reached around and unzipped the back of it, flinging it to the ground. Derek's mouth descended upon my breasts, his other hand pressed into my back, holding me in place as he encircled my nipples with his tongue. Heated flickering pleasures quaked within.

I panted. "Ah… Can I come?"

He cupped my face. "Yes. Let this be one of many orgasms you'll have tonight. I need you as relaxed as possible. Come here, lay in my arms and come on my hand, just like you did the first night we were together." He shifted to his back and I curled into him. "Remember that first night? You opened up and let go?"

I peered into his eyes. "Yes."

"That's what I need you to do for me tonight, just let go." I nodded and spread my legs wide for him. "So good, baby."

Two fingers glided back inside, ramping me back up to the crest. His other arm held me tight while his mouth alternated between my lips and my breasts. He frothed me into a sultry fever as I bucked and bounced on his hand. His fingers found my engorged clit. He tapped and rubbed it until my sluicing juices squirted like a sprinkler.

"Oh fuck, yes!" I cried.

"That's it, sweetie, just come. We're going to get all wet and messy tonight. Let it out."

"One last stream punctuated my geyser-like release.

Derek lowered his lips to mine. "God, you're incredible."

"No. It's you. You unleashed something inside me that I didn't know was there. Now I feel like the places you can take my body are limitless."

"That's because there are no limits to the pleasures we have yet to discover. With you, with us, the sky is the limit."

"Sometimes I feel like I'm walking on air when we're together like this—like my body is soaring."

His index finger grazed along my jawline. "I feel that too."

I jerked on his shirt. "You're still dressed."

"I was just thinking it's a little hot in here, with you still in your garter and stockings, and the fire."

"Get naked and join the party!"

"Of course, my sexy little minx. Then I'll tend to you."

Derek undressed in a flash. His cut, long, powerful frame never ceased to bring me to arousal. He knelt down between my legs, removed my heels, treating me to a blissful foot massage.

"Oh my God, your hands are like magic. Don't stop… Ah…God."

"That's the same thing you say when I'm massaging your pussy."

"It just feels so good, you have no idea. Can I make a marriage vow right now?"

"I'm intrigued, so yes."

"If you vow to rub my feet everyday, I vow to love, honor, and suck your dick all the days of my life."

He busted out laughing. "Done and done. In fact, I insist." He switched feet and smiled down at me in that sweet, loving way that lit me up from the inside out. "I'm looking forward to taking care of you for the rest of my life. I want to give you the world."

"I want to take care of you too, but I can't give you the world. I can only give you all of me."

"That's everything I ever wanted." He gathered me into his arms.

My legs snaked around him and his hands splayed on my back. For just a moment, we locked eyes before he gently took my mouth. With open lips, the tip of his tongue joined with mine and our kiss deepened, reaching my heart's center. His rigid erection rested at my slick entrance.

I maneuvered myself to take him inside and he stopped me. "Sweetie, the next time I'm inside you, I'm claiming you fully. Let's get you ready." He patted my bottom. "Stand up for me, I haven't finished undressing you."

My body fused with electricity as I stood before him, obeying his wishes. His proficient fingers undid the front clasps of my stockings. "Turn around."

I submitted to his request and he unfastened my stockings, sliding them down in a slow scintillating fashion that left a trail of goose flesh. The garter was quickly discarded and I felt his hot breath wash over the small of my back. "Now bend over and let me see."

I flexed forward in a hot second with renewed moisture trickling from my slit. Derek's fingers spread apart my quivering flesh.

A low growl escaped from his throat. "Fuck, I can't help myself." He immersed his face into my pussy and my knees buckled beneath me. On all fours, Derek nourished himself on me from behind with zest. The man had an appetite for my pussy and was satisfying his craving. His velvety tongue worked me over at maximum speed. Then his fingers rammed inside me turning me into a heap of twitchy soaked glee.

His voice vibrated on my clit. "God, you taste delicious. I want to taste all of you. Lay on your tummy."

I flattened, wondering what he hadn't tasted… Oh…oh…oh… *Come all ye faithful!* Really? My body tingled in anticipation as his tongue drifted over the curve of my butt and slid along my taint. A twittering spasm of delight erupted inside. He pulled my cheeks as far apart as they would go and tickled my taut rosebud with his tongue. This wondrous new decadent sensation overtook me as Derek lavished me with luscious licks. My body hummed toward the cusp.

He granted me a soft bite on my bum. "I'm going to need you to come for me one more time before I take your ass. Can you do that for me?"

I moaned. "Yes. I want to come again."

"Lift your hips, a little bit."

I inched off the comforter and presented my wanting cunt.

"That's a good girl." His fingers went to work skimming my hot spot, making me squirm. "Who's pussy is this, Nia?"

"Ah…it's yours. It belongs to you."

"What else is going to be mine?"

"My ass. Oh…God…my ass will belong to you too."

A wet finger pushed into my ass and my orgasm fractured apart and singed through me. I screeched a string of wicked fuck cries, dousing Derek's hand in my pleasure juices, until my body disintegrated and melted into the comforter.

My heaving chest rose and fell in satisfying exhaustion. "Oh, Derek, that was amazing…and…I…"

He smoothed the hair off my face and smiled. "I know. You're ready."

"I'm ready."

"I love you, Nia."

"I love you too."

He grabbed the lube, coated his finger in it, and it slipped easily inside. He circled his oily digit, preparing my walls for his cock. I released quiet moans, excited to give him all of me. It was the moment of truth. Derek lifted my hips and his tip pressed against my puckered ring.

He exhaled. "I can't do it like this." He swept me up and angled me to face him. "I need to be able to see you. It's your first time. It's our first time. I need your eyes on mine."

"I want that too."

"Come here." He pulled the cushions off the couch, stacking them together, and got on his back. Then he guided me to straddle him. "You're in control, Nia. I don't want to hurt you. When you want more, bear down on me. Understand?"

"Yes. I understand." I picked up the lube and reapplied it to Derek straining erection.

He blew out an appreciative breath. "That's my good girl."

I reached around and steadied his cock at my tightest opening. Our eyes transfixed on one another. I eased myself down slowly and the first few inches of his cock crammed its way inside.

I stilled for a moment, relishing his presence and gasped. "Oh, it's good. It's so fucking good."

"Yes, baby. God, look at you. You're beautiful."

"You're beautiful." I panted. "And I want more."

"Breathe and let go. Just like the first time we were together. Open up for me."

I exhaled and managed to stuff half of his massiveness inside. Once my body allowed the girth, I gently rode him up and down. This intoxicating intensity took me on an odyssey of ecstasy. The circuit of energy that flowed between us united on a deeper more intimate level.

"You're doing so well, baby. You feel amazing."

He dipped two fingers inside my wringing wet cunt. This eclipsed anything I'd experienced before. I longed to be packed fully, so I gradually tunneled down on Derek, and took him nice and slow, while he stretched me. My ass squeezed his cock like a boa constrictor, revving up our burning desire. He couldn't take it any longer. He clutched me to his chest, drew his knees up, and thrust into me to his balls. I wailed in raw carnality with my head on his chest.

He slowed. "Sweetie, look at me? Did I hurt you?"

My eyes met his. "No. I'm okay." I breathed through the pain. It only hurt for a second. "It's good. I'm letting go, just like you taught me."

His thrusts were steady, but easy. "That's my baby. You're incredible."

"Ah…ah… I'm totally and completely yours."

"Yes, Nia. You're totally and completely mine."

The intensity grew with each tiny movement of his fullness gliding along my anal walls. "Oh, God…ah…I want you to come inside me.

He pressed his lips to mine. "Yes, angel. Eyes on me."

He stroked me with pure benevolence. It was like flying too close to the sun, without getting burned.

Derek was tender, yet powerful as our bodies built to release. We strained and moaned together, grappling to hang on to our euphoria.

He wedged a hand between us to finger my clit. The abundant impact of his fingers and his masterly cock was too much. "Oh, God, Derek. I'm going to come." I dug my nails into his shoulders. "I can't hold on any longer."

He clasped my face. "Don't hold on, sweetie. Let go. Come for me."

My orgasm gripped me, racking me to pieces. It splintered through me in currents of tormenting pleasure. Right before Derek came, he crashed his mouth to mine, with powerful dominion. Yes, I was his totally and completely.

He growled and gritted through his teeth. "I love you, Nia."

I cried out in a whimper, "I love you, Derek."

His forceful release staked its claim, as his creamy cum pulsed inside me and overflowed. He clamped onto my hips, holding me in place until the last cathartic peak of our ultimate fulfillment.

My head collapsed on his chest. His arms cloaked around me in a firm embrace with his lips nuzzling my ear. "Baby, you were exceptional. I'm proud of you." He slowly extracted his cock and eased me on my back. "You amaze me." He brushed my cheek with the back of his hand. "You took all of me on your first try. You're such a good girl."

I beamed. "I had a really good teacher." I grazed my fingertips over his chest. "I fucking loved it."

He chuckled. "You have a very dirty little mouth, Miss Kelly." He touched his lips to mine. "I fucking love you. So, do you want to camp out down here tonight? Spend our last night as single people, sleeping in front of the fire."

"That sounds perfect."

"Okay. Let me get cleaned up, get some more pillows and blankets, and then I'll be back to take care of you."

"Sounds like a plan."

"Do you want your wine?"

"Yes, please."

He handed me my glass and kissed my forehead. "Be right back."

I sipped my wine and giggled to myself in contentment. Derek was right—we got deliciously messy. What a transcending experience. Instead of going the traditional route and spending the night apart, I opted for butt sex. Tradition could kiss my cum-soaked ass.

Derek returned to the living room, loaded down with supplies for our sleepover in front of the fire. He put down the blankets and pillow, and then knelt down next to me, washcloth in hand. "Can you turn over for me, sweetie?"

I put my wine down and rolled onto my tummy. "I was just thinking, since I didn't spend the night at your parents' house, I broke with tradition."

He tidied me up with the washcloth. "Yes. It was a very naughty thing to do."

"I guess, I'll be a bad girl for the rest of my life."

He delighted me with a kiss between my shoulder blades. "I'm counting on it. There. All done. Let's get you on dry land."

I scooted off the top comforter and Derek put a fresh one in place. Then we snuggled under the blankets.

I took my regular spot with my head on his chest. "I might be too excited to sleep."

He held me a little tighter. "Just try, for me, baby. Tomorrow's a big day."

I whispered, "I can't wait to marry you, Derek Pierce."

"I can't wait to marry you, Nia Kelly. Now, close your eyes, angel. Go to sleep." He kissed the top of my head. "Goodnight, my sweet girl. I love you."

Chapter Sixteen

"You're going to be a beautiful bride, Nia. My son's a very lucky man." Charles, Derek's dad, embraced me warmly.

I was in the bedroom with Valerie. The hair and makeup people had just gone. My dress still hung in the closet and I donned a blue satin robe that Julia had given me before I left Las Vegas.

"Thank you, Charles." I said, "I think I'm pretty lucky too."

He patted my hand. "I wish you nothing but the best, and lots of babies."

"Charles," Valerie scolded. "She's not even down the aisle."

"Fair enough. But wouldn't you agree, Nia and Derek would have beautiful children."

She kissed his cheek. "Agreed. Now, you might want to go check on our son. He may have put on a brave face when we got here, but deep down, I think he's a nervous wreck."

"You're probably right, my dear." He turned to go and stopped. "I know you're going to make Derek very happy, Nia. Welcome to the family."

I smiled. "Thank you, Charles."

He left and Valerie took me by the arm. "Come sit

with me for moment, Nia. I have something for you."

We sat on the bed and she reached into her purse and pulled out velvety box. "I wasn't sure what Julia has planned, but I wanted to make sure you had something borrowed and old. Charles gave me these earrings on my wedding day. You can wear them today if you like." She handed me the box.

I opcned it. "Oh my God. They're stunning."

"I checked with Derek. He said they would go beautifully with your Bulgari necklace."

"Yes. I don't know what to say. Thank you." I hugged her. "So, was Derek really nervous?"

"A little. I think he's more excited than anything. I'm excited too. I'm so glad you'll be a part of our family. And as your soon to be mother-in-law, I'd like to make my vow to you."

"You would?"

"Absolutely. I vow to love you as one of my own. To not butt in, as much as humanly possible. And if you and Derek have an argument, I vow to always take your side."

I laughed. "Really? I don't know that any other mother-in-law has said that in the history of mothers-in-law."

"Well, I know my son. And he's exactly like his father if his feathers get ruffled."

"Oh? I had no idea."

"What's that you kids say, 'Fear not, sister, I've got your back.'"

I cracked up. "Valerie, you're so hip."

"I try. Anyway, just so you know, I'm here for you. As a friend, as whatever you need. You're the perfect woman for my son. You're strong." She squeezed my hand and rose from the bed. "Well, I better get downstairs and check on things. The minister should be here soon."

"Thank you, Valerie. Thank you for everything. I'm so glad you're my family."

She cupped my face. "I am too, dear."

No sooner had Valerie left than there was a knock on the door.

"Best man and flower girl, reporting for duty." It was Keith and Tim looking dapper in their tuxedos.

Tim hugged me tight. "How's our bride holding up?"

"I'm fine. I'm just a little anxious for Julia to get here. I hope they didn't get stuck in traffic. Are you really my flower girl?"

"No. That was a little joke we had with Derek last night at happy hour. No one is supposed to be prettier than the bride and steal her thunder, so I better not."

Keith laughed. "As if. Come here, gorgeous." He wrapped me up in a big embrace. "I'm so happy for you two."

"I'm so happy you guys are moving to Las Vegas. I'll get to see you almost every day. You'll be like family."

At the risk of getting too emotional, Tim chimed

in, "Well, there goes the neighborhood. Be careful what you wish for with Keith. He'll be raiding your refrigerator every day."

"All I'm going to find in Nia's fridge is kale and cheese. Don't worry, baby doll, your refrigerator is safe with me."

"We should go check on the groom." Tim kissed my cheek. "We'll see you at the altar. Congratulations."

"Thank you. If you see Julia downstairs, will you send her up? And, tell Derek, I love him."

Keith smiled. "You got it, girl. Consider it done."

I checked the clock. In just one short hour, I was going to walk down the aisle and marry Derek. The butterflies kicked in. What if I can't remember my vows?

The bedroom door opened. "Is someone looking for the maid of honor?"

I squealed, "Julia, you made it! I'm so glad. I'm getting nervous."

"Why? Your hair and makeup are flawless. I've never seen you with your hair up. You look like a sexy princess."

"Are you kidding? You're the sexy one. That coral strapless dress looks double fabulous on you. Oh, and by the way, since you're married, you're not the maid of honor, you're the matron of honor."

She put her hands on her hip and pondered. "Okay. I see where you're going with this, and I'm going to have to veto matron."

I giggled. "God, I wish Steve and Scott were here. They would have a field day with matron, Julia."

"Have you heard from them?"

"Oh yeah, we've talked a lot since we moved into their old house."

"Did they say anything about their Christmas plans?"

"Not really. I assumed they are spending it with family."

"Hmm…that's interesting." Julia sauntered to the door. "Because if you had talked to them today you would've known, they're here."

She flung open the door and Steve and Scott marched in.

"Oh my God! I can't believe it. Oh, I think I'm going to cry."

Scott elbowed Steve. "And, you owe me twenty bucks."

They greeted me with firm embraces. I collected myself and asked, "Steve, what about your dad? It's Christmas Eve. Shouldn't you be with him?"

"Dad is fine. We've had some good news. He's responding to a new treatment. The doctors are confident this will not be his last Christmas. After everything you went through with Larry, we had to come. Derek arranged everything. I'm so happy for you two."

"I'm so glad to see you. Thank you."

Scott held up his left hand. "Nia, you're not the

only one who tied the knot. Look."

Julia grabbed Steve's left hand. "Did you guys get married?"

Steve blushed. "Last week."

We erupted into a chorus of cheers. In fact, we were so loud, we barely heard a knock at the door.

Scott volunteered. "I'll get it."

"If it's Derek, send him away," Julia replied. "We don't want any bad luck."

"Hi," Scott said softly. "Yes. Of course it's okay. Come in."

We all glanced at the door. It was Brooke. I couldn't believe my eyes. I engulfed her in a hug with tears in my eyes. "Brooke, I'm so happy to see you."

Those were the only words I could get out before I cried in her arms.

"Hey. No tears. It's your wedding day."

"I'm sorry. I'm so sorry about everything. I never should've…"

"Nia, I'm sorry too. I keep thinking if I hadn't left, I could've somehow protected you from Shannon and Larry."

"Girls," Julia interrupted. "There's no crying. We're celebrating today. Not just Nia and Derek, but Steve and Scott just got married too."

She greeted them with warm hugs and reached into her big bag. "Well, then, it's a good thing I snaked this from the kitchen." Brooke held up a bottle of champagne. "I didn't grab any glasses though."

"That's okay," I said. "We'll pass it around, hobo style."

Brooke popped the cork. "Oh, Tom's downstairs. He wanted to see how Derek was doing. And, I hope you'll think this is good news. We're moving back to Vegas. The new owner of the country club, Adam Maxwell, made us offers we couldn't refuse."

She handed me the bottle and I raised it in the air. "This day keeps getting better and better, and I'm not even married yet. Okay. I want to make a toast to the four of you. When Julia helped me start over, you all rallied around me and helped me begin again. So, to my peeps, my family, my TV binge watching gang, I salute you, and I love you."

I took a sip and passed it around. The room grew quiet for a moment.

Brooke handed the bottle to Julia and she waved it away. "Oh no thanks. Someone has to stay sober and redo Nia's makeup and get her into her dress."

"We'll go downstairs and let you get ready," Steve said.

Scott picked up the bottle. "Yes. We should, but the Veuve Clicquot is coming with me."

Brooke gave me a reassuring squeeze on my hand and they all headed out.

"Julia, I think you will have to fix my makeup. Brooke gave me the surprise of my life. Did you know they were coming?"

"Yes. Derek arranged everything. He really loves

you so much."

"I love him too. I feel like all the ups and downs were badges of honor that we had to go through to get here today. We're finally free from everything. Sorry to go on. Leave it to me to babble away. I guess I'm nervous. Can you help with my makeup?"

"You might want to give it a moment."

"What are you talking about?"

There was a faint knock at the door. "I'll get it," Julia said. "You should probably sit down."

Sit down? I was getting married in a half hour, but I flopped down on the bed anyway.

"Nia," Julia said. "This is your Christmas present from Derek."

"Merry Christmas!"

I popped up. "Aunt Mary Jane! How are you here right now?" The tears spilled down my cheeks and we embraced, shaking with emotion. "I thought you couldn't come. What about Uncle Bill? Is he still recovering?"

She led me back to the bed and we sat down. "Well, he and I got to talking and he wanted me to come. He said you needed to have family here today. And of course, Derek is also very persuasive."

"But, it's Christmas Eve. Who's taking care of him?"

"Oh, who do you think? That old bag Ann Benson couldn't take over nursing duties fast enough."

I laughed. "I don't know, Aunt Mary Jane, it

sounds like she has a thing for Uncle Bill."

"Well, as long I was able to come and be with you, she can bring him all the fucking sweet potato casserole she wants."

Julia howled, "Aunt Mary Jane, I could listen to you drop the f-bomb all day."

"Yeah, she gets that a lot." I patted her hand.

"Well, I know you've got to get your dress on, but I just have one thing I wanted to give you before I go." Aunt Mary Jane reached into her purse and pulled out a laminated index card. "It's my secret recipe for Mac and Cheese. And now it's yours."

"Really?" I hugged her again. "Thank you. I've been waiting for this."

She grinned. "I know. I gave a copy of it to your mother on her wedding day, and now it's your turn. You're marrying a man who loves you the way you deserve to be loved. I know your mom and dad are so proud of you."

"Thank you. That means everything."

She kissed my cheek. "I love you."

"I love you too." She rose from the bed and I grasped her hand. "Aunt Mary Jane, wait. I need to ask you something."

"What's that?"

"Would you walk me down the aisle?"

Tears pricked her eyes. "It would be my honor. I'll let you get ready, and I'll be right outside the door waiting for you."

She left and in a frenzy. Drill sergeant, Julia helped me get ready. It was time.

She stood behind me in the mirror and clutched my hand. "Nia. You look beautiful." She choked back tears. "I'm so happy for you."

"Oh God. You can't cry. I'll start crying again. Julia Dickson, I expected more from you."

"I can't help it. When I think of how many times I almost lost you... And now, look at you. You're marrying the man of your dreams."

"Are you sure that's all? It's not like you to be so emotional. Are you okay?"

She pursed her lips together and nodded. "I'm better than okay. I'm pregnant."

"Oh, Julia. That's the best wedding present you could ever give me."

"It's happening, Nia."

"What's happening?"

"All those things we talked about in college. How we would stay up late and dare to dream that one day we would have a family, a real family, where we belonged. You and me, we're finally getting everything we ever wanted. We belong."

"You're right. And we did it together. You're my sister."

"You're my sister too. Now, let's get you hitched."

＊ ＊ ＊ ＊

As I floated down the aisle to Derek, I clasped onto Aunt Mary Jane and a bouquet of Stargazer lilies. The room glowed with candlelight and the distinct smell of Christmas permeated the air.

The second my gaze locked with Derek's, a lump formed in my throat. He was my husband, my forever, my destiny.

Aunt Mary Jane gave my hand in marriage to Derek and he kissed her cheek. We faced each other in front of the manger scene and he mouthed, "You look beautiful. I love you."

Fireworks went off in my belly as I drank in Derek's incredible ice-blue eyes filled with love for me. I barely heard the minister say, "Dearly beloved, we are gathered here today to witness the union of Derek Pierce and Nia Kelly. I was told the couple wanted to say their own vows."

Derek took my hands in his. "Baby, your vows?"

"Oh… I–I…" I trembled with emotion and tears flowed down my cheeks. "I'm sorry."

He wiped away my tears with the pad of his thumbs, and said softly, "It's okay, my angel. Do you want me to go first?"

I nodded—"Yes. Please"—and glanced down.

He tucked his finger under my chin and tilted it to meet his gaze. "Look at me, sweetie. Eyes on me."

I blew out a shaking breath. "Yes."

He gave me that smile that embraced my heart and held me to his soul. "Nia, I promise you in my arms you will always be safe and protected, and I promise you in my arms you will always find family and love. And, my beautiful sweet girl, I promise you, in my arms, you will forever be home."

THE END

Nia and Derek's journey continues in:
Derek's Christmas Carol
A seasonal novella for Christmas…

Author Biography

Rosemary grew up in Pennsylvania, one of six children. Her parents, Charles and Dorothy, always supported all her creative endeavors, from acting to singing to Erotic Novelist. Yes, they are super cool.

She's been living in Las Vegas for over eighteen years with her husband Bill Johnson and their rescued pooch Harley.

In addition to writing, she also teaches ten fitness classes a week. Her limited spare time is usually spent at home with her hubby enjoying a home cooked, healthy meal and all things HBO and Netflix. When she ventures out to a restaurant, she normally splurges on her favorite dish, Mac and Cheese. It's just like Nia says in the Swept Away series, "Sometimes it's good to be bad!"

ROSEMARY WILLHIDE

Lightning Source UK Ltd.
Milton Keynes UK
UKOW02f1855130415

249572UK00001B/46/P